ESCORT UNLEASHED

THE EMMA SERIES, BOOK TWO

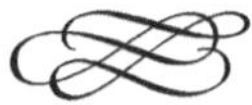

JAMES GREY

CONTENTS

I

I squeeze the soap-drenched sponge and watch as a delta of white wetness splays out from where I hold it at my collarbone. Then, like a river in reverse, the streams gather as one, and run down the gap between the triangles of my breasts. I see the river gaining momentum as it takes off towards my belly button. Cleansing that which cannot be cleansed. No, mere soap will never purify my wanton flesh.

I don't know why I'm holding my breath like this. It's about the fourth time I've caught myself staring dumbly down at my body. I don't understand how I can be doing this. I can't believe my world has changed so much in a month. The young body I'm surveying from on high, warm shower water leaping upon its surface like hundreds of cackling, opportunistic little tropical bugs, is about to go on sale.

I shudder, and I'm not sure what that means. My hand wants to guide the coarse sponge down my torso, to lead it across my left breast. I let it. The rough surface catches my nipple, and it's no accident. She responds — I can feel her rear up, erect as a cowboy on a horse — and I shudder once more. This time I know exactly what it means.

My head is hanging weirdly, and I've been in the shower for, what, twenty minutes now? It's like I'm trying to get cleaner than I've ever been before. I tell myself not to be silly. That triple-washing my skin isn't going to cancel out the dirty deeds my flesh will commit. I don't seem to be listening. Maybe I'm enjoying it too much.

In my mind, I keep replaying things that haven't happened yet. In just a couple of hours from now, a limousine is due to arrive in the street beneath my apartment. A professional driver will take me to my first assignment. I will be spending the night in Notting Hill, with a man called Charles. Martin's friend Charles, to be precise. This is the man who sponsored me through my training. Now that I am qualified, I am in no doubt as to what he will want from me. I have known that from day one.

And tomorrow, I am assured that I'll be receiving five thousand Pounds in my bank account. Before midday.

I am so wanton.

I am so wanted.

This time tomorrow — unless I chicken out — I'll have become something new. A woman who sold herself to a pleasure-seeking man. There is only one word for it: I will have become a *whore*. Once that money lands, that will be it. No turning back the clock. I'll be a hooker forever. Once is enough for the label to stick.

I hang up the sponge and soap my hands with my creamy, frothy citrus-scent body wash. For the umpteenth time, I glide these hands up and down my sides, then along my arms, and I can feel nothing but glowing warmth. A pleasant little tickle as I gently trace my nail on the inside of my elbow, where it's always been deliciously sensitive.

My body feels so alive — now of all times! Somehow, I want it to feel desensitised and detached. I want to be as far removed from my physical being as possible. I'm not sure Miss Jackson would agree.

She'd say detachment would make me a Petra. I sigh. There's no detachment she'd have to worry about right now. The reality of this moment would no doubt please my shameless mentor from training: I think I'm stuck with being a horny Emma today. Good for business. But bad. Oh, so bad.

Under my arms it tickles more than usual. I got fully taken care of today, and not just *there*. Oh no, not just there...between my legs it's smooth as an ostrich egg. Just a tightly mown runway remains. And thanks to the latest laser technology, which I'd never even heard of, it didn't even hurt.

I'm told the treatment was cutting edge, state-of-the-art. It must have cost a fair whack, I should imagine, but apparently that's no concern of mine any more. Lucy booked me in to a place in Knightsbridge that treated me like royalty. I wouldn't have been surprised to see Princess Kate herself emerge from the next-door treatment room. I breathed a sigh of relief when they confirmed that the account really *was* all taken care of. It's almost a month since I quit the day job, which means I've now become acquainted with that choking feeling that I'll be missing a pay cheque soon. My bank account is pretty sickly.

Cash shouldn't be a problem after tomorrow, though.

My soapy hands spread cleansing goodness all over my thighs, inside and out. I let them explore my butt too. The flesh of my cheeks feels soft but toned. Twenty-six. I'm at the absolute peak of my womanly life. I'm experienced and emotionally mature, yet still as beautiful as I've ever been. I feel sexy.

I can't make up my mind if it's a good or a bad thing that my first appointment isn't a complete stranger. Someone I've met a couple of times. More seriously, that it's with a friend of one of my closest friends. I think that with time I can come to terms with just about everything in this job, but I'm not sure if looking Martin in the eye will be one of them. I haven't brought myself to do it since coming back to London from the school two weeks ago. We've spoken on the phone, and I was way too shy to go into much detail about my training. But I don't think I'll get away with putting off a face-to-face meeting after tonight. He knows that Charles will have me first. And he has some sort of right to know how I'm doing, I guess. It was Martin's idea that I explore this path. If it's really going to lead to pots of gold, then I owe him a drink or two.

Wouldn't it be better, though, if it were totally incognito? Would I feel more scared or less scared? More like an unfussy East End harlot, or less? Probably 'more' in both cases, but on the other hand I wouldn't have to worry about people I know hearing of my wicked deeds. London is a huge city, but I'm still terrified to think that I'm doing this in the same town where I grew up. Home. The place where I have friends, family and ex-colleagues.

I shake my head in confusion as I turn and let the water splash me in the face, closing my eyes as I imagine what Charles is going to want from me. Yes, actually, I think on the whole it's better that my first call will be to someone I've met. I've got enough first-day nerves without having to deal with a weirdo. I'm pretty sure Charles is decent and sensible, otherwise he wouldn't be friends with Martin. And I know he's good-looking. I keep having flashbacks to the way he gazed at me when I met with him and Lucy in Mayfair. I'm having another one now, and I feel myself begin to sway a little. I have to steady myself with a hand against the shower door.

I have some notes on what to expect. Working for Lucy is a professional experience, to the point of being surreal. My very first agent (it sounds impossible that the word 'agent' has anything to do with me) ran through everything on the phone with me this morning, and couriered a printed copy of the assignment to my door shortly afterwards. It's enough to make me want to clean myself down there, just one more time. It feels so good to feel my soapy fingers gliding between my legs while I recall her promising words.

"I don't want to spoil your first assignment by telling you too much," she said this morning, her tone such that I could almost hear her beaming at me over the phone. "And the only reason we can have that luxury is that I know you won't get any unpleasant surprises. Charles is a sweetie, you know that already. He's different in a private situation, of course, but there'll be nothing not to like.

"As I think you know, he does want to spank you. It won't be anything terrifying. From what I've seen in your school report — and I trust Miss Jillings completely on these matters — you'll cope admirably. In fact, although I'm sure you'll be nervous, I think you'll find time to enjoy it."

I still can't extinguish the images she ignited with those words, even all these hours later. I still can't help feeling that washing my hungry labia with my finger like this, perhaps straying onto my clit now and then — just to be quite sure it's clean, of course — is only making them wetter, which will make me need to wash them again. I sigh and wonder if I'm ever going to escape the vicious cycle of this inflamed shower.

"He's not into anything weird," she continued. "He likes to worship a woman, revel in her. He knows it's your first time, of course, and that will be a gigantic turn-on for him. Several of his peers would have been happy to outbid him for the pleasure of having you first, but he sponsored your schooling. And when that's the case, there's an etiquette amongst the London gentlemen."

I love the bald feeling I've got down there, and marvel in its hairless slickness. I tug at the tight hairs of my little patch, then try to find the tiniest hint of hair anywhere else, but I get nothing. How I wish I could see! I imagine being photographed, legs wide open, poster girl for the fancy salon…and a current of pleasure surges through me.

Calm down, brain! I force my curious, wandering hand away from my nether regions and hope that washing my hair again will cool things in my head. The array of high-end cleansing products, scents and body washes that arrived on my doorstep this morning was mind-boggling. I chose the intriguing champagne conditioner for my mane. You could almost convince me to drink the stuff — really! It actually says it's a *limited edition* from Moët and Chandon. Who knew they licensed hair products? It's on a level of quality I can barely comprehend. I'm not sure I can ever go back to the super-market stuff now.

"He's booked you for the whole night," I recall Lucy concluding. "You'll be staying over at his house and, essentially, you'll be his wife until breakfast tomorrow. You don't have to worry about prying servants because he doesn't believe in them. He will treat you like a bloody princess. I'm pretty sure you'll forget it's a paid assignment before very long at all!"

And with that she wished me luck, told me not to cut corners on my grooming (no danger of that), stressed there was no need to overdo makeup given my 'natural sensuality' and reminded me to look out for the dress Charles picked out for me. It would arrive by courier in good time this afternoon. Who knew there were so many delivery guys in London? I've spent half the afternoon opening the door to a steady stream of polite, uniformed men bearing mysterious packages!

I think about how sweet and supportive Lucy has been since I got back from the school. We've met twice for coffee, and she's fielded every question I could possibly throw at her with an informed, smiling, reassuring manner. She told me she was thrilled with my report card from the school and that she wanted me on her books. She never put any pressure on me or rushed me, and before a week went by I ran out of reasons to protest.

I turn the water to cold as I rinse my hair. I need a drop in temperature.

Lucy's only request was exclusivity: as long as I was with her, I was not to work with any other clients or agents. I was more than happy to keep it simple and work with someone like her. I gave her my word five days ago, and we sealed it with a handshake. I could stop any time I wanted, even after one client. No nonsense, no contracts. I find Lucy Fulford implicitly trust-inspiring.

After that, she set about lining up my appointment with Charles. I've been on edge ever since, and particularly since I got in the shower this Wednesday afternoon.

But the chilly water is doing the trick — the oldest cure in the book! I'm calming down just a little now. My nerves level off as I finish rinsing my hair and finally turn off the taps. I think I've got my lust under control for the moment.

I immediately begin to wonder if that's a good thing.

I need to be ready at six. I believe we'll be having a leisurely dinner first, with Charles as my chef. Odd, really, after the no-strings sex I got used to in training. It does sound a lot like a date. I hope Lucy's right, and I can put the whole payment thing out of my mind.

My mental preparation seems to be working, I think to myself as I grab one of the horrible cheap bathroom towels I bought from the local supermarket and start to pat my flesh down. I've been good, and doing what Miss Jackson advised: meditation and porn. The combination of guilt-reducing self-hypnosis, a regular diet of sexy viewing and no actual sex — after all, I have no boyfriend as such — has undoubtedly got me hornier than ever as my first appointment approaches.

There's still some doubt and disbelief, but surely that's to be expected. The nagging voice that insists on reminding me how disgusting all of this is has been dimming, although I can hear it a little louder today. It sounds vaguely like my mother. Which is odd, because she's never spoken to me about sex at all.

I expected that angel on my shoulder to be there, of course. Let's see if it disappears once the first client is out of the way. The voice doesn't like it when I use the word 'client'. It's stark and it leaves you in no doubt. The angel wants euphemism.

So there's that, but there's also *need*. Boy, did I get spoilt at the school. I've taken care of myself a few times with my porn home-work since getting back, but it's not the same thing as being with someone. I've been so hungry that I've even toyed with the idea of calling up one or two of my old flames whom I know would give me a good seeing-to. But I decided against it for the same reason I've been avoiding seeing my parents and my friends. There would be questions, and I'd have to spin a web of lies.

What I want to do is get through this *client* and make sure I'm really going to keep doing this. Then I'll take the time to think about whether I'm going to attempt to hoodwink everyone I know on a long-term basis. I shake my head at the thought and make for the bedroom.

There's a massive pile of clothes on the floor. As promised, the school delivered everything from the vast closet I shared with Petra. The only problem is that I don't have a walk-in wardrobe here. There's nowhere to put all the stuff. I *suppose* I might be able to afford somewhere a great deal more spacious by next month. If my, er, *performance* is good. And if the sums I've been hearing about aren't some kind of practical joke. Part of me still thinks they must be.

Right now all I need to worry about is the dress laid out on my bed. It's an elegant black number, with a reasonable knee-length hem. Two wispy shoulder straps will hold it in place. On the whole it looks quite respectable, like something I could wear on a night out. I doubt it's something I could afford, though, I think as I slide the fabric between my fingers and thumb. No, definitely not! You don't get silkiness like that in the places where I've gotten used to shopping.

I check my notes, and there are no instructions about underwear. I shrug to myself, figuring just about any of the stuff from my lingerie drawer at the school will do. Something about the turquoise set grabs me as my eye roves the stack of skimpy bras and panties at my disposal. It's bright and bold, yet lurid in the classiest way. There's a beautiful twirly cream and black pattern around the top edges of the cups and panties. I try not to think too much about Charles lowering them with his teeth as I put them on.

Soon I find myself dressed and ready to go. I select a little handbag and consider what I should take. My purse, of course. Fresh underwear is a must too. My mobile can come along, but I suppose it ought to be on silent. I decide to do that now so that I don't forget and embarrass myself later. Just as I flick into quiet mode, I get a vibration.

It's Miss Jackson! I remember now. My mentor and I traded numbers before I got on the train to come back to London. It's a text message.

Emma Carling, you gorgeous girl! Little bird tells me you're off on your first job tonight? Just wanted to wish you luck. You are going to knock their socks off for sure. Enjoy it, and enjoy all the dosh ;) Let's catch up soon xx

She really does have a knack for timing — how does the woman do it? I'll probably never know. But hey, her message is most welcome right now. It calms me to hear my decidedly hands-on teacher has such confidence that it's all going to go smoothly. I hammer out a quick reply, realising as I do so that I haven't let my friends from prostitute school know that my D-Day is here. We've all been slack. I really must get in touch with the gang soon.

I put away my phone, ready to focus on entertaining. I stand up and brush myself down. One final check in the mirror. It's a fact: I don't think I've ever felt so stunning. I think he's going to be pleased.

Then, for the fourth time today, I jump as the buzzer from downstairs sounds. My heart skips a beat and my stomach curls around itself. This is not another exciting delivery. This will be my driver. *Fuck – this is it!*

I am about to become a prostitute. I take a deep breath and step out of my door.

II

e's already taking my breath away. I'm kneeling on the floor of his bedroom, near the foot of his king-sized bed. In keeping with his wishes, I'm upright and leaning slightly forward, so that my bare knees take my weight, pushing hard against the chocolate-marble carpet. My hands rest demurely on my thighs, twitching fingers and all. My feet are shoeless, and the unmistakeable fabric of the black dress blankets them as it swishes gently around my heels.

And I'm thinking, *this is it.*

Charles, the man who paid for me tonight, stands tall in front of me. We have dined and conversed, but now, I, the consenting adult, have allowed myself to be brought upstairs for reasons I understand very well. He led me up to his room with a gentle, reassuring grip on the fingers of one hand. I followed with my heart thumping off the charts.

It's still going crazy now, somewhere beneath my breast. It feels like it might burst through my rib cage with the next beat. I'm teetering on the knife-edge of no return now. This perfect gentleman would let me go right this minute if I asked. No charge. No mark against my name.

But I am asking for no release. I am too turned on for that.

I'm a grown, independent woman. I have the right to have chosen to be here. I have the right to say what I am saying. And I am saying yes. I am saying *fuck yes!*

Not one of the twelve days I spent at training prepared me to feel excitement like this. I am so aroused that it hurts. My sharp passion is burrowing away at my guts with a scythe. He is a sexy man, and he has treated me handsomely this evening. Lucy was almost right to say that I might forget this was an assignment. But not quite. It's in the back of my mind that he's paying thousands of Pounds for me. It sounds like an impossible exaggeration, but it's not. He is *literally* renting me for a four figure sum.

It's in my mind that this is my first time being taken. Paid for. Owned.

It's in my mind that he *knows* it's my first time. This man who sponsored my training. I have a blazing desire to pay him back with every sinew of sexuality I have.

There's a magic buzz around my head that I don't think I've felt since my very first date, long before I was even a woman. The anticipation is unbelievably powerful. It's like an invisible wire attached to my scalp, crawling with static and hitched to the ceiling.

I don't know where to look. I'm fixating on his beautifully tailored brown trousers, and the thighs within them. He is still fully dressed. A light blue shirt, open at the neck, and a smart pair of brogues, complete the picture. He's told me to kick my shoes off, but apart from that I am still dressed in the black outfit he instructed me to wear tonight.

I can feel the wetness melting into my expensive panties as he takes a step nearer, so I can actually smell that scent of his — the after-shave that screams wealth — and he takes my chin in his hand. He lifts my head so my eyes meet his. I feel them roll in their sockets. I'm a little drunk. Some of that is alcohol. But most of it is need.

"I love you like that, Emma Carling," he murmurs. "Kneeling there just like that. Here in *my* bedroom. All for me. It makes me feel so very lucky to be alive. You are beautiful and I am blessed."

I swoon. Why does this man feel the need to pay for sex again?

"I am going to enjoy every moment of you tonight, Emma. I want to welcome you to a world you will never want to leave."

He murmurs these words as if he has all the time on earth. And he does, I suppose. I don't know if I should say anything.

"Are you a nervous girl?" he says, tipping his head disarmingly to one side.

I nod. And I feel I should speak. A new voice — one that sounds a lot like Miss Jackson — whispers that I'm supposed to be showing the excitement I'm feeling. But I don't think I'm getting that right.

"It's okay, my sweet," he whispers. "It's okay. It's your first time. I've initiated women before and this is normal. I can see that you are aroused. It's enough for me. You don't need to say anything if you don't want to. I understand. I want you to enjoy."

I swallow hard, closing my eyes again as his index finger tickles the soft skin of my throat now. Somehow I remember to nod again. I'm sure he's right when he says he can see I'm aroused. His words are driving me crazy. So is kneeling here in front of him. So far below him. I am his little plaything.

When will we really begin? My mouth is dry. We haven't even kissed yet.

Charles is speaking again.

"I want to undress you. Do you realise that there is no amount of money in the world that can buy a second first time with you? The magic of finally undressing you and seeing your perfection unveiled…is literally priceless. The only bank I can store it in is my memory bank. And yet I can think of no greater treasure."

I hadn't realised.

I feel overwhelmed by these things Charles is saying. They're unbelievable, but his sincerity is billowing through the room with the same intensity he's got in his eyes as he speaks to me. I'm staggered. How can my naked body be worth so much to this man? It's all a bit much.

And I whimper: "How do you know I will be...perfection?"

I can hardly splutter out that word, and my voice lowers to almost nothing as it escapes my lips. I was brought up to be modest. Yes, boyfriends have thrown the 'perfect' word around before, but did they *mean* it like this guy does? £5000 says he means it. I flush hot at the thought, and it's not the money itself. It's knowing that I'm worth that much to him. It's scary.

I hear his voice somewhere in the distance, dreamy yet rock-certain. "I know you will be. I knew it the first time I saw you, my sweet. I am an art lover, Emma, and I had that rare feeling of staring a masterpiece in the face when I first laid my eyes on you. And you are worth a dozen Mona Lisas to me."

His finger pauses again and I tilt my head back, entranced by the moment and his words. Charles is positively oozing charm and praise. He doesn't *need* to! He is paying a king's ransom for this. He can call me demeaning, disrespectful names. He never needs to see me again. And yet...listen to the man. Could there ever be any truer words spoken?

The foggy depths of my memory remind me that he's chosen, openly, not to marry anybody. He hand-picks beautiful women for his pleasure, no more. Oh, but the way he speaks...he could make any girl his own! My God, and yet he's paying for *me*. Of all the girls in London! And so *much*. My head spins.

"Stand up now, my beautiful," he says, breathing in deeply and removing his hand from beneath my chin. I rise to my bare feet, as elegantly as I can. The floor and the carpet still feel hard beneath them. My knees are a little red from the kneeling, I think. But he's only looking at my eyes. And I'm mesmerised by his.

"I need you naked. Would you rather undress yourself for me, or have your clothes taken off you? You don't need to say it. Show me."

I'm puzzled, wondering what he means. But my body responds before my brain can process anything. I feel my arms rising above my head, like I'm getting set for a high-dive.

I guess that's his answer. What I want is to be stripped. What I want is to cede everything.

His breathing quickens as he takes in my response. He allows himself a moment's pause, then gets down on one knee. Is he going to propose?

Christ, I think it would be a yes.

But no, he's lightly gripping my ankles with his long, handsome fingers. He's cupping them with his hands and now they're rising up my legs. Like their master, they are in no hurry. They linger, but they don't wander. They travel straight up, the thumbs deftly reeling in the hem of the dress as they climb above my knee.

My arms are still raised in the air as he journeys tantalisingly along the outside of my thigh, and then over the tiny speed bump of the panty string on my hip. I can almost feel his appreciation of my skin flowing back into me. I feel so desired that I might faint.

The dress is coming with him now as I feel his warm palms make their way up my hyper-sensitive sides, his thumbs sailing noiselessly over my ribs. The dress tickles my stomach as it dangles its way up, and then it nuzzles my nose as my bra is revealed and he completes the removal of the black garment. When he slips the last of it over my raised wrists, I am sure I have never been undressed so willingly.

Charles stands back and looks at me, standing there in the turquoise and cream bra and panties, as I drop my arms down to my sides. He flicks the dress away to my left, down the little hallway of his hotel-style bedroom. Not once do his eyes leave me. They are beginning to flash now. In a good way.

I toss my head, letting today's new hairdo wake up. It taps me on the shoulders and my fingers seem to be clawing desperately at the flesh beneath my hips, where they happen to be hanging. My body is aching with a need for touch. Another new feeling.

He whistles softly as finally his eyes leave mine and they rove the length of my body. Up, down and up again. He walks slowly around behind me, pausing close enough for me to feel his breath. But there's no touch.

The weird thing is that Charles is making me feel as special as I've ever felt on a *regular* date. I wasn't ready to be bowled over like this. It's almost like…romance.

I can't take it anymore. I just can't. He is close behind me and he needs to know my need. I bend over. Right over. Hands on my ankles over.

I didn't plan this. One minute I was standing there obediently, the next I'm offering him access to my sex, just a yank of my sodden panties away. *Fuck!* Did I really just do that?

"Do things like that, Emma," says Charles, whose shoes I can see between my ankles, "and speaking will be absolutely surplus to requirements. You're communicating your arousal to me very well."

Stupidly, I redden.

"I am thrilled that you are a hungry girl," he goes on evenly, walking around back in front of me now. "I knew you would be. But you need to wait a little longer. Undressing you is absolutely sacrosanct. Keep up the enthusiasm, though, and I may have to delay your spanking and proceed to other important business."

I stand up straight again, all reluctance. I think my mouth is gaping. Do I want a spanking, or do I want fucking? Oh God, too much choice! He's smiling at me. And now he steps forward, brushes a couple of strands of loose hair back behind my ear, and kisses me deeply.

I melt. Was it supposed to be this good?

I'm hungry for his mouth and his tongue, and it feels so warm, so wet, so good, the way he's feeding my need. I try to kiss him back but he dominates our movements, controls where my tongue will go. Truly, it's fine. He's making me shiver with what he's doing, especially when he pushes his tongue in so *deep*. So hard and yet so soft.

I think I'd kill to be this guy's wife. It makes me feel light-headed to think that he wants me this much. The whole thing is intoxicating. My apprehensions have vanished and all I know now is that I have never felt so much like a woman.

He takes it slow, and my eyes close as we kiss. I've been expecting this to feel like some kind of awful, dirty prostitute kiss. One that counts for nothing but shame. But instead it feels pure, normal and natural. In fact, it's better than any I've ever had. Because I can feel his power almost flowing into me. Because I have no questions about where this is going, or what it's for. I think I am coming around to his way of thinking about the opposite sex.

At last he stands back, removing his hands from my shoulder blades. He takes a very deep breath and closes his eyes, almost as though he is about to enter a trance. Is he preparing for a religious experience?

"You are ready for the final part of your undressing," he murmurs after a long pause, his voice softer than ever as he opens his eyes. "I want to undress you many times in my life, Emma Carling, and each time I do so I will be grateful to be on this earth. But I can never repeat this first time."

I gulp. He really has a thing about this. And then I nod. *Mmm.* First time. Oh yes, it's special for me too.

"Turn around please, Emma. And remove your bra."

His tone is less controlled now. The breathing is getting heavier. I reach around behind me and unclasp the bra as instructed. Following his every instruction feels the most natural thing in the world. This is a side of my character that's only recently introduced itself to me.

But the part of myself that I know better wants to take initiative, too, and I hook my thumbs into the panties, ready to remove them. In truth, I can't wait to be naked before Charles.

"Tsk," I hear him. "Wait a moment. I want to run my eyes over your back. It's so beautiful in this light. I want to admire the way your sides rise and fall when you breathe; the swooping curve of your shoulder blades; the sheer artistry of your soft, toned muscles. The contrast of your dark hair and your milky skin."

The man is a poet, and I am helpless at the brute, dazzling sincerity of his words. I drop my hands again, aching with desire at the thought that he's admiring me in such detail.

"Now," he says after a minute or so. "Stay facing away from me, and remove your panties. I would like you completely naked."

I do as he asks. And I feel a powerful ripple of thrill run through me as I stand up straight again, my twitchy hands at my bare sides and my underwear on the floor.

There's a long silence. I wonder if he is meditating for real this time. I become aware of the clock ticking in the corner. And then some soft music fills the room. Tranquil panpipes. He must have a remote control or something. The sound comes from nowhere and everywhere. This is definitely no cheap sound system.

At last, Charles speaks again: "All right, Emma, I'm ready to see you revealed in just one moment." He pauses, as if gathering himself. "You may turn around."

And I do it. He's sitting on the bed, looking earnest and utterly absorbed in the woman in front of him. That £5000 girl who is...*me*.

I don't know what to do with my hands, so I leave them at my sides. I don't want to look a show-off. Again, he says nothing. He just closes his eyes for a long time, as if unable to comprehend or take in what he's seen. When he opens them, he seems surprised to find I'm still there. Very slowly, he shakes his head.

"Better than perfect," he whispers, just loud enough that I can hear him from three paces away. "Come closer to me."

I step towards him, stopping just in front of his knees. His hands remain on the mattress, leaving his eyes to do all the work. They travel from my own eyes to my chin to my collar bone to my breasts, where I see them dart from one nipple to another, and then back again, and then all the way down my body. He repeats the exercise several times.

"Pure," he says. "Pure like Eden."

I could get used to this kind of worship.

He stands up suddenly, giving me a little fright.

"I'm not going to spank you," he announces, still not laying a finger on me. "I cannot stomach foreplay when you've aroused me for this long. I want to lay you out on my bed and fuck you. Right now."

Sounds good to me. I'm not sure I'll survive foreplay in this state either. Not without calling on a few of those delaying techniques I learned at Cranleigh House.

I just smile at him, because he makes me feel that I can. He smiles too. I know he knows what I'm thinking.

"I'm going to lift you, sweetie," he says. "Fall into my arms."

I let him take me, his forearms beneath my thighs and shoulders. He's strong and I feel deliciously vulnerable as he makes light work of laying my limpness down on the duvet that covers his bed. It feels so soft and delicate against the skin of my back. The room temperature is impossibly perfect. I'm neither hot nor cold. It's perfect for sex above the blankets.

I'm not sure what to do, exactly, as he moves around to the foot of the bed and begins to loosen his belt. So I do what I want to do. Which is to open my legs for him. I bend my knees a little, feeling my heat rise as I display my craving sex to him. He looks pleased.

"I will inspect that beautiful little pussy of yours at close quarters after our first orgasm, darling, don't worry about that. Right now, I'm going in."

Our orgasm? He's no Rupert, this one. I like him better for it.

I can't wait, especially now that I can see him freed from his trousers. He looks incredibly appetising, and his arousal is plain to see. I think I know exactly what that means for me.

Then he crawls onto the bed, lowers himself gently onto me, placing one hand behind my head and easing his cock into my relieved, inflamed vagina. I sigh. He starts to kiss me again. I didn't think I could yield any more to him, but as his tongue takes hold of mine and his torso presses against me, every inch of skin and muscle boiling with hot need, I find myself letting go on a whole new level.

I try to part my legs even wider. I'm frustrated that they can only go so far. The very act of throwing them open, to be taken after what feels like a long drought, almost makes me come. My back arches and I know we're as close as we can be. Pressing hard together, connected, all the way from his palm on my hair to our relentless kiss and his nose on my cheek, down across his heaving chest flattening my breasts and then, finally, to where he's actually inside me.

For all that I sensed he had cracked and wanted to get down to business, he's still taking it slow. I think he's still in a spiritual place, entranced by me. I'm there too now, inside a bubble where it's just me and him. Where the centre of my universe is nothing but his manhood in the centre of my body. He's not pushing yet. He's revelling in the being there. I can feel his enjoyment growing by twitching degrees. He's shooting larger every few seconds, like one of those time-lapse videos of a flower coming to life.

"I want to do everything to you all at once, Emma," he whispers, a trace of frustration in his voice. "If I had five mouths, I'd use them all right now."

All I can do is moan my approval. I can barely handle his one mouth right now. I'm torn as he leaves my lips, but then I'm groaning once more as he moves to kiss my neck. It's soft and sensitive there, and while his lips caress it his other hand brushes my ear, gently pulling and twisting my earring. It turns me on to be touched there.

I can't keep my hands on his shoulders any more. He's made me go too limp with lust. My wrists fall down on the sheets, my arms mirroring my splayed legs as the fingers scrabble mindlessly at the fabric of the pillow-case. I'm feeling surges of something I've never felt before.

"Charles, I can't...please..."

It's getting too much. Something so volcanic is building inside me that I don't think I can contain it much longer.

His cock twitches and expands again at my whimpering beg. He knows what I want, and his control is ebbing away too. The animal grunt of his response, which is a million miles from well-spoken Charles, tells me that much.

Then, thank God, he gathers pace. And he fucks me like there's no tomorrow.

III

I think I made a fool of myself this morning.

He wanted to make me breakfast. I know he would have done a good job of it, if last night's home-made wild asparagus soup and poached salmon was anything to go by. I was hungry after a night of endless play. And I didn't really have anywhere I needed to be.

Plus, I like the guy. I mean, what's not to like? He can cook like a champ, he's sophisticated and respectful, he's powerful and wealthy, and he makes a whore feel anything but. The man licks pussy with the gusto of a starved jackal, yet with the soft, repetitive touch of a patient artist's brush on canvas.

He made me come three times last night. As I lie on my bed at home now, still clad in that impossibly soft black dress, feeling tired and a little peckish, I can't help smiling at the memories. Especially of the unbelievable first moments on his bed. That was pure, one hundred percent erotic fantasy. He walked us both slowly to the edge of heaven. Then, once he started to go for it, we were both there in less than one explosive minute. Charles will not be needing Viagra any time soon.

Later, after he explored every inch of my body with his mouth, I came helplessly at his tongue's touch. And then again, sometime in the sleepy greyness of dawn, we curled together and I found myself tickling my own bud as I leant over him and took him in my mouth. Then he took over, licking my ass while he used fingers just where I wanted them, and I climaxed with a jolting jerk.

I felt wonderful as I drifted off once more, but when I awoke to full sunshine and the birds chirruping outside his window, I felt embarrassed to be there. There was a knot of tension in my stomach, for no good reason. It's like something inside me was concerned that I liked it so much.

I was polite to Charles and enjoyed a cuddle with him, but I felt a little distant. I told him I needed to get back home. He seemed almost to be expecting that. He just smiled and said he understood, and the chauffeur appeared in a quarter of an hour. I avoided small talk as I put my clothes back on and freshened up, but we kissed as I left. He said he hoped to see me again soon.

And now I don't feel happy or sad, just kind of satisfied and kind of lost. And sleepy. Yet my mind is a little too busy for sleep.

I know exactly why I'm satisfied, of course. But I'm lost because I expected to be more uncertain about things today. Shouldn't I be wrestling with more guilt? Instead, I almost feel at a loose end.

Is it going to be this easy? Am *I* going to be this easy?

The fact is, I didn't feel much like a prostitute last night. And it's confusing. I shake my head and stare up at that skylight I like so much. I think back to the last time I flopped on my bed after work: the day I walked out of that evil corporation and its made-up consultancy shit that isn't even a real thing. That crazy day feels like a lifetime ago. I am something else, somebody else, now. I've done the deed and I've got this feeling it's too late to go back.

Which is nonsense, I know. But I can't help the broodiness this morning. I'm really quite tired. I should fix some breakfast, but my body wants sleep more. It's adamant and it knows what it needs, even though my mind is confused about what to feel. Fact is, after a night like that, I'm used to obsessing over where things are going with the guy concerned. That's not even a question that makes sense any more. What would Miss Jackson say?

Just as my eyes begin to fall, my cellphone peeps rudely from the bedside table. It's a text. I reach over and peer at the message with the one eye I feel energised enough to open.

Holy fuck! Suddenly I'm wide awake and sitting bolt upright. Both eyes fly open when the words on my little screen register.

It's a message from my bank. £6000 have been deposited.

I blink at the screen, counting the zeroes — yes, there are *three* of them — and trying to take it in. Christ almighty, I'd forgotten all about the payment! Lucy has been as good as her word. Money in the bank the next morning, she said. But wasn't I getting *five* thousand? Where did the extra come from?

I'm just about to float to the living room and look for my assignment notes to double-check my fee when my phone does its thing again. This time it's Lucy.

Well, well, well, somebody did something right last night ;)
£1000 tip...you GO girl!! Bet you're feeling weird, but...coffee
this afternoon? x

Coffee *now*! That's what I need. Of course I'll meet Lucy later, but I'm positively reeling at the moment. I feel a bit dizzy as I get up off the bed. The money...none of it seemed real until this moment. But now it's actually in my bank account. And the tip alone is half a month's salary in my last job.

It seems so unreal that I don't want to trust the text message. I click through my online banking app until I get to my account balance. Then I truly believe. The total has never started with a six before. At least not with so many digits kicking around behind it. It all adds up. The transaction is complete. Slowly, incredulously, I suck in the stale air of my ageing apartment. I can't quite take it in.

This has blown my confusion away for a moment. I'm just overwhelmed by big-money talk actually turning to real cash. I keep shaking my head and muttering the words 'six thousand…' in disbelief as I make my way to the kitchen, feeling every kind of wobbly, and put the kettle on. I don't know what's frying my brain more, the fee itself or the grand tip. I knew there were rich people in this new world of mine, but…no, I simply can't process it.

I spoon some instant coffee powder into a mug. It feels weird being a millionaire — well, compared to anything I've ever known, I am — and drinking instant. Weird in a cool way, I think to myself as I stare uncomprehendingly out of my kitchen window, slowly sipping on the ghastly brown no-name supermarket liquid.

As the coffee slides down my throat, so the sunny reality begins to seep into me. This could be my last mug of instant for a while, I smile to myself. I don't need to live like this anymore. My eye falls on the hipster coffee joint across the street, which I've always had to avoid unless I want a treat. I figure that I might just start getting them to deliver me a large latte every morning. And I think I'll have an almond croissant with that, too.

Lucy is beaming at me as she takes a sip of her cappuccino. I've taken care of the drinks this time. The woman gave me six grand this morning. Least I can do.

"All right then, Miss Carling! You're the apple of my eye at the moment! Seems you can do no wrong. You do know I'm going to want all the details."

"Oh, I was afraid you were going to ask me that!" I giggle. This morning's confusion has vaporised and now I'm in a thoroughly good mood. Hot sex and tons of cash…why exactly was I worried again? "Well, I suppose I can hardly decline, since I'm working for you!"

She nods, still smiling. "This is true. I thrive on feedback. This is how I keep my clients happy and any new girls informed about what you need to do. For what you girls earn, a full run-down isn't much to ask for."

I shrug, and nod confidently at her. She's right, of course. Like Miss Jackson, there's a wisdom about her that is compelling, disarming and not remotely arrogant. It's a thin line to walk, and they both walk it well.

"So, did he spank you in the end?" she enquires, leaning forward.

"Come to think of it, he didn't!" I reflect. "I'd forgotten about how that was supposed to happen."

"You got caught up in the moment, didn't you, you minx!" she teases. "Bet you've got quite a few things jumbled up in your head!"

"I guess *he* got caught up in the moment too," I say drily, "if he abandoned his well-laid plans."

"He wouldn't be the first!" she laughs. "Do tell me more."

"Okay, well, he made a big deal about undressing me," I say, lowering my voice a little, though thankfully the café is pretty empty. "He did it really slowly, and then I had to turn around while I got out of my underwear. He seemed to go into a bit of a trance for a while."

She nods thoughtfully. "Ah, that sounds like our Charles. And I bet he was a pretty thoughtful lover, wasn't he?"

I redden. "Uh…you could say that. At first it was pretty straight-forward, once he put me on the bed…just…you know…but then…he did stuff with his tongue…"

I'm struggling. You just don't talk about these things where I come from.

She puts her hand on mine, which is fidgeting awkwardly about the table.

"You'll get used to talking about these things, don't worry," she says. "Let me make it easy for you. He fucked you hard and then he licked your pussy till you exploded. Am I right?"

I nod, relieved that's all I have to do. And even then I don't catch her eye.

"Blowjob?"

"Yes. It was all quite natural, to be honest. It was sort of like just being a normal couple. It wasn't like 'do this, do that' or anything."

"You'll be surprised how often that will happen, Emma," she grins. "Just because these men use escorts doesn't mean they're all depraved or domineering, although as you are well aware some of them will be. But I'd say more than half of them just want a 'girl-friend experience'. And from what I can gather, you provided exactly that last night."

She reaches into the side pocket of her laptop bag and takes out a printed sheet, which she lays on the table in front of you.

"I shouldn't really be letting you see this, but I know encourage-ment is good for you right now," she says. "This is an email I got from Charles this morning. Like I said, feedback is everything, and many of my gentlemen are happy to provide it. Some of them find it quite a turn-on to write a little report card. Isn't that funny?"

I give a little laugh, although I'm a little more uptight than she is about what I might be about to read.

Dearest Lucy,

Emma Carling...oh my, we weren't wrong! This girl is one in a hundred. Perhaps even one in a thousand. I loved her. I abso-lutely loved her. Please don't let her go, ever!

Her perfect body and angelic features are something we've discussed often enough. I don't need to tell you that seeing her disrobed was perhaps the most beautiful moment of my life.

I will spank her next time — probably — but last night I was simply overwhelmed by the desire to worship her. Not only is she stunning, but she has a certain X-factor I can't quite place. Maybe it's her veneer of innocence, which is utterly genuine. I hope we can preserve it, whatever it is.

But what stands out most for me is her wonderful responses. Sleeping with her — and I do mean sleeping, as well as every-thing else we did — felt as natural as sleeping with a true lover, even a wife. She was in it with me from the beginning. As lustful and as hungry as I was. I could feel her need throughout the night, and though she was always willing to follow instructions, I loved that her natural quest for pleasure made everything flow so well. In truth, I didn't feel moved to give her orders very much.

Of course, I had a slightly awkward lady on my hands this morning. But as you know, this is quite normal for a first-timer and I found it charming in its own way. I loved that she felt a little bit wrong about doing what her deepest instincts had led her to do, and that she'd had so much fun in spite of herself.

All in all, I think this is some of the best money I have ever spent. It was my privilege and my honour to take her first. Thanks, as always, for your outstanding mentoring and prepa-ration of the women that you send me.

Yours, Charles

She is watching me intently as I try to suppress a smile by averting her gaze. I don't come close to succeeding.

"Hey, you're allowed to smile!" she jokes. "You couldn't have hoped for a more glowing response, could you?"

"I suppose not," I say, with a bashful shrug. Meanwhile, my heart is leaping with excitement and pride. And this time, I haven't forgotten the money in my bank account. If this is what people think, and that's how fun things are, and that's what I can earn... how could a girl not smile?

"Well, Emma," she says, sitting up straight and businesslike. "I'm

hoping that as it went so well, we can make this an ongoing relationship and keep working together."

I'm struggling to think of the tiniest reason why a girl would
walk away from £6000 text messages the morning after a night of
fine food and finer sex. And I'm drawing a blank. She senses it.

"If you're willing to stay in this game, we'll need to do a few
things. I will fix you up with a personal hair and beauty specialist
whom you will see on a regular basis. I can arrange you gym
memberships and dieticians at no cost if you want. I don't insist on
these things, however, as I trust my girls know how to keep themselves looking good. Everyone is different, and you in particular
seem to need very little interference. Mother Nature has blessed
you."

I'm going a bit red again.

"We will also need to do a photo shoot with you, much of it
nude," she goes on. "Many of my clients want to see what they are
getting in great detail, if you know what I mean. Again, for the
money you get, it's not much to ask. And it will only make your
stock go up. Bigger tips, probably!"

She winks at the last statement. I sense she has more to say.

"Where spanking and the like are concerned, I will be easing you
in. I am well aware that you can withstand — and more important,
enjoy — further punishment. But some time soon, we'll need a
special session that establishes just where your limits are. I don't
want to throw you to the wolves, so to speak.

"Finally, I'll need you to spend some intimate time with a couple
of the other girls on my books. No doubt you'll be in demand for
group work, and I can't have you working with girls you've never
touched before. Like you, these girls are natural bisexuals and I am
quite sure you will share an animal attraction to each other. I think
you'll have a great deal of fun.

"Not all nights will be as easy and natural as last night," she says,
her speech drawing to an end. "Your time at Cranleigh House has
prepared you for that, I am sure. I can assure you that all your nights

can be just as much fun if you let them, and I'm happy to proceed with further assignments right away if you're in agreement. Over to you, Miss Carling."

I have a vague sentiment that I should be outraged by the nude photo shoots, the sado-masochism and the enforced lesbianism. Prim, English Emma really should be. But who am I kidding? Not only am I willing to do those things, but I'm painfully aware that I'll almost certainly enjoy them. Concerns about my reputation among people close to me linger, but I know they began to be overpowered when that text landed this morning. I'll handle that side of things, somehow.

I breathe in and sit up straight like her. "I'm in, Miss Fulford." She sticks out her hand, and we shake on it.

IV

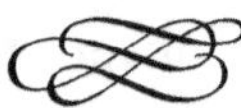

For the next few days, there's a lot for me to get used to. My new-found wealth, for one thing. And the fact that I'm in London, not inside the high hedges of Cranleigh House. This is a city where I actually *know* people. Sooner or later, I need to think of what I'm going to say to them.

There's only so long I can keep questions and social meetings at bay, and finally my excuses begin to run out. I absolutely have to see my parents. I haven't completely ruled out being honest with them in the future, but part of me thinks I might yet run away from this new life, or do something wrong and get fired. And then I won't have to tell anyone anything. I'd be able to just bury this little secret in what will become my past.

I'm fooling myself and procrastinating, I know. But I'm going with the delaying tactics for the moment.

So I don't breathe a word about my new career as a whore when I go round to my parents for dinner. Thankfully they don't ask too much about my 'trip to a remote Greek island' — although I have to fib about a camera malfunction to explain my lack of photos. After that, my father takes over the conversation, regaling us with stories about *his* trip to Greece in the sixties. For once, I'm grateful for his capacity for delivering long-winded yarns.

I tell my parents I'm looking for jobs, but there's nothing too exciting to report just yet. Everyone's cutting back. Recession's hitting hard. Well, at least those things are true. I keep my statements general and vague, because I don't much like lying.

My mum is concerned about how I'm going to survive in the meantime, and offers to lend me some money. "And you're always welcome to come and live with us for a while," she smiles.

My stomach turns at the thought of one of those chauffeurs turning up at my mother's door to whisk me away to another wealthy client. I can honestly think of no worse nightmare. The thought crosses my mind that I'd rather have my bare ass whipped by a succession of ugly millionaires until I bleed, but I hound it away quickly. I assure my folks that I've got savings, and I'd rather not be dependent on Mum and Dad. Plus, moving my stuff would be a massive pain.

Speaking of which, I've got some pretty risqué clothing lying around the floor of my apartment now. I'll need to be careful with visitors. That, or move in somewhere with a walk-in closet. But how would I explain a fancy new apartment when I'm supposed to be jobless? Oh God, there's so much I haven't thought about.

Nor can I entirely avoid the girls from work — or ex-work, to be precise. They drag me out for some cheeky cocktails one Tuesday evening, and they pepper me with questions while I try to stop myself giving the game away with airy offers to pick up the tab for everyone. I have to keep turning the conversation to the electrifying circumstances of my departure, and thankfully they're more than happy to reflect on that. Those who missed my fiery exit have heard the stories on the office rumour-mill, and everyone seems to approve.

I'm assured that my ex-boss was seen deep in conversation with our CEO that day, and that she has been noticeably more circumspect since. While the latter is something that gives me a lot of pleasure, making me feel I left a legacy that might make life better for my successor, the mere mention of the CEO has my heart thudding. I hope my face doesn't give away my concerns about Mark D. Spurring.

Did he recognise me the last time we were in a room together? *Does he know?* Has he told the whole office that he saw Emma Carling at the hooker school where, every so often, he secretly lectures new groups of initiates?

I scan the faces of my friends as I ask what I hope are casual questions about his lordship, who has thankfully always been a regular conversation topic amongst us. Not least for his dictatorial ways, but also for the unavoidable reality of his knockout looks.

I'm hoping I'll spot any signs that the girls are keeping something from me as we discuss him. I can't see anything in their eyes. Good! And it figures. I didn't think Spurring could give me away without giving himself away.

Come to think of it, I'm still getting a salary from my old job. The bank notification for that deposit paled into insignificance in the face of that text following my night with Charles, but nonetheless it came as a surprise. As I sit there with my friends, the thought crosses my mind that Spurring might very well be more worried about me knowing his activities than the other way round. Maybe my ongoing salary is him trying to keep *me* away from making any trouble about my departure.

Then again, maybe Accounts just screwed up. It wouldn't surprise me, they're fucking useless after all. So I'm still none the wiser about whether Spurring knows or not. But at least my ex-colleagues don't. Yet. Thank God.

I know that if I tell one of them, I've as good as told them all. Again, I can imagine a time when I might carry this 'escort' label with the pride it deserves, and tell the lot of them what it is that I do. I feel pretty sure at least half of them would be envious, though they'd never admit it.

I really shouldn't be holding back, but my Englishness makes me keep my other life secret. For now, anyway, I'm sticking to the line that I'm meeting job agencies but I'm not just going to take the first thing that comes along. I'm even dropping hints that I might go travelling.

Not a bad idea, that, actually. I could just tell everyone I know in London that I'm going round the world for a couple of years, while in fact I stay home and ply my trade. But then, knowing my luck, I'd bump into somebody on the tube. Even in a city of close on nine million people, it happens. And more often than you might think.

It's not that I'm not dying to talk to someone about it. In many ways I feel that someone should be Martin. But not just yet. He wants to meet me, of course, but I've been honest in telling him I need a couple of weeks. The thing with Martin is that he knows too much. He's aware that I've serviced his friend Charles. He won't press me for much detail, I dare say, but if I meet him I'll feel obliged. We've always shared everything.

I'm just not ready to talk to a man about all the finer points yet, even if it is the man to whom I owe everything for sending me down this path. He's almost infuriating in how understanding he is. Frankly, I'm a bit pissed off with myself for not seeing him right away. I owe him more than a few drinks, and what's more, he's the one person I don't need to lie to.

Yet the person I eventually contact is Sarah. Who better to share things with than a girl with whom you shared a room – not to mention bodily fluids – during training? She's still living outside of London, but I text her a few days after my début night.

Hey Sexy! My God, I did it! First client last week. Sooo hot!
Looks like I'm going to stick at this. Want to tell you all about it.
When you coming to look for work in London? Come get wet
and rich with me! Xx

She's thrilled for me, of course, though I feel bad for wanting to gloat about how much I made. I know she's struggling financially.

Then again, maybe she needs some motivation to join me on the dark side. I know she needs a confidence injection to really go for it, even though she passed training.

Ooh, smoking news! Good money, huh? Well, that should get me off my ass, huh! That, and kissing you again ;) How about next week, then? Xx

I'm thrilled to think of her coming to London. She's been on so much of this journey with me, and it would be great to have her around for these exciting first few weeks. Plus, I love the thought of sleeping with her again.

Just say when, gorgeous! You're staying with me. I'll move over in my bed...but only a little ;) And I'm paying for everything till you find work. Xx

It's funny what a good, giving mood all this has put me in, but there's no reason I can't be generous now. Especially to my first girlfriend, or whatever she is. I've really begun to miss her. I wondered if the whole thing with her was just an experimental holiday fling, but it doesn't seem like my heart has bought into that explanation.

Sarah's visit arranged, and with Latifa and Alyssia also making noises about heading to the capital soon, I have even more reason to be cheerful as I take on my second and third clients. They're not quite so lucrative, but it's all relative. Three grand is still decadent pay for a couple of hours' work! Still well above what I used to clear for a month.

Lucy assures me that I'll have plenty of big nights again in the future, and pay will vary. She's easing me in with 'vanilla' clients, and that's part of the plan. "You're doing straight sex with easy customers on these first few calls," she explains on the phone. "So they're paying a fairly standard fee. Once you get into servicing groups, intense anal and bondage, for example, you might be looking at even bigger sums than you got from Charles."

I feel a little tingle down below when she mentions intense anal and bondage.

"And once word really gets around about you — and believe me, it's happening already — even straight sex could result in bidding wars. On certain weekend nights, for example, a few clients might want you, and then we'll send you to whoever offers the most. And you'll be surprised how silly these men become when it comes to a fat-wallet competition. All of which has you and me laughing all the way to the bank!"

Although I only have a couple of clients in the couple of weeks after my thrilling, erotic debut with Charles, Lucy is in constant contact and she keeps me busy with some of the other things she mentioned.

We establish a highly flexible availability diary, which allows me plenty of holiday time as long as I give her two weeks' warning. She lines me up with a personal stylist, Hannah, who will take care of everything from my pussy patch to my nails to my eyebrows on a weekly basis. She works at the same parlour I visited ahead of my first assignment, and it looks like that's where I'll be spending my Tuesday afternoons from now on. Not much of a chore, especially since Hannah does massage, too, and Lucy insists I book one whenever I want loosening up. And it's all on the agency's account.

It's amazing how life goes. After all these years, the moment I can afford to pay for massages is the moment I get told they're all on the house. I feel like fucking royalty. The notion of giving all of this up starts to make less frequent appearances in my head.

I pass on the gym for now, but I use my leisure time — of which I have plenty — to take lengthy strolls along the river. It keeps me vaguely active, and reminds me just how much I don't want to go back to spending my days sitting in a chair in front of a screen.

I do have an interesting meeting with the dietician, just so I don't do anything silly. I'm getting into thinking about food a little more, especially now that I'm able to afford all those ridiculously expensive little delicatessen touches that go into recipes. My kitchen is already filling with things I never contemplated before: Himalayan rock salt, truffle oil, saffron and pine nuts. Maybe I'll try making Martin dinner when I finally feel ready to see him.

The nude photo shoot is enough of a thrill that I have to go straight home and use my vibrator afterwards, especially as the dreamy, long-haired photographer catches my eye several times while I expose myself to him and his lens. If Lucy wasn't there to direct proceedings in person, I'm not sure something wouldn't have happened between me and the photographer. But the whole thing, which involves a lot of lacy lingerie changes, is empowering, sexy and a lot of fun.

More so because I trust Lucy to guard the photos with her life. Even clients, she assures me, are required to meet her and view prints if they want to see photos that show my face. The digital versions would never be sent anywhere, so the chances of a leak are slim to none.

Lucy also puts me through my paces with three of the other girls on her books: Tracy, Samantha and Carla. She does it properly, renting a hotel room and supplying plenty of champagne. Tracy, an American blonde with what must be the most kissable lips on the planet, seems to hit it off with me. Lucy is impressed with our natural intimacy and how we make each other come more than once. She especially likes how we both completely forget the audience.

All this seems even easier than I could have imagined after the challenges of the school. It seems like no time at all since I would have been desperately apprehensive in these situations, but the school and my homework is beginning to bear fruit. As for an attraction to women, I'm beginning to suspect it's always been there. It's just that now I'm allowing it out. Thanks to Sarah, I guess.

Am I cheating on Sarah, though? It crosses my mind…but the thought is a silly one, really. Whatever we want to call our relationship, we're both going to be fucking a lot of other people if all goes to plan. It's work. Even if it feels a lot like play.

As for my second and third clients, they're not as memorable as Charles, but they're fun outings. I'm not required to spend the full night with either of them. One is an Arab sheikh, whom I entertain at his Kensington residence, and the other is an English businessman who insists on picking me up in his Aston Martin and taking me to a weirdly cheap hotel room.

He drives fast enough to scare me, but he's not very demanding on the sex front. Curiously, he only asks me for a blow job, which ends with a hot gush in the back of my throat, and then he's done. I don't even have to undress, but the whole thing makes me so slick and horny that I ask him, blushing but shameless, if I can finish myself off. He smiles and says, "Good girl...I love your spirit. Please, be my guest."

And he watches me climax with my skirt around my hips, a glow on his face, before driving me home well ahead of midnight. There's a handsome cash tip from him too.

I think it's fair to say I'm getting pretty comfy with the vanilla sex. The sheer naughtiness of it, plus the joy of the act itself, plus those beautiful texts in the mornings...it's a trio of thrills that has me in love with my life right now. Can it really be this easy?

V

I know that we're somewhere in leafy south-west London, but apart from that, I'm in the dark. Quite literally. We've been blindfolded since the moment Lucy picked up me — and then four more of her escorts — in her own car, took us to her stunning apartment overlooking the River Thames and gathered us in her living room.

Lucy was in an unusually tense mood from the beginning of the evening. She told us this wasn't a job in the traditional sense. She told us, with a deadly serious face, not to even *try* peeking. We'd lose our fee for the night if we did. Apparently we're dealing with a well-known personality. One who would take no chances with privacy. Hence the enforced blindness.

None of it made much sense to me. All I could say was that losing sight is incredibly disempowering. And I wasn't alone in that. The girls were extraordinarily quiet as we were led to a car and taken on a half-hour ride to…somewhere.

That was around eleven. Now it must be really, really late.

I'm on my knees, curled up in a tight ball, my forehead on the floor and my buttocks on my heels. Oh, I'm completely naked too.

We were stripped — I don't know by whose hands — the moment we entered this place. And I have no idea where my clothes are now. For all I know, we're all being photographed for the front page of *The Sun*. Powerless doesn't begin to describe it.

We're being given instructions by a woman. Her tone is even and serious, almost like she's a computer. Yet she speaks with a husky, soft voice, and has a foreign accent I can't quite place. I'm picturing her as a kind of exotic Esmeralda. I hardly dare breathe when her commands are given close to me.

The few clues I've gathered suggest that the room is a big one. Though we're on carpet — or maybe it's a rug — right now, we walked some distance across rough wooden floorboards to get here. At one point I felt the warmth of a fire on me, and I can still hear its crackle and spit somewhere not far away. There's a slightly musty smell to the place.

Though the woman I'm calling Esmeralda seems to be in charge of proceedings — and hers is the only voice I hear — I am sure others are present. I had hands steering me when I needed to move. One pair was large and male, I think. It guided me into position with a light hold on my shoulders, before releasing me upon the woman's instructions.

She refers to each of us by our names. Carla. Teresa. Melissa. Katarina. *Emma.* We're told to take tiny steps until we're exactly where she wants us. It appears that she's very serious about getting us into a straight line before she instructs each of us to adopt the position I'm in now. I think that two of the girls are on my left, and two on my right. I must be centre stage.

Esmeralda tells us we should continue to maintain strict silence until otherwise instructed. Then I hear the woman murmur something I can't quite make out — it possibly isn't English — and heavy footsteps begin to march away from us. The shoes beat the floor in time, like it's the military. I'm picturing uniformed men. Why are they leaving, and what are they leaving us to?

I hear a heavy door close behind us, and the marching feet slowly fade from my hearing. I assume Esmeralda is still with us, but there's now absolute silence in the room. The only interruptions are the odd spark from the fireplace, and the creak of a floorboard as someone shifts their weight. I still don't know if there might be others present. Maybe there are people who have been there since we were brought in.

I wish I could look across to my colleagues for some kind of reassurance. I am sure they must be feeling the same apprehension I am. Blindfolded and stripped, in an unknown place, nobody could feel remotely at ease. Yet I know Lucy would never, ever, send any of us anywhere dangerous. I trust her, even though she said she wasn't permitted to give details of this unusual assignment.

The only thing I do know for sure is that none of the other four girls in our party have done this particular call-out before. We're all relatively new starters.

The silence persists for an abnormally long time. Without my phone and my watch, I'm clueless as to how long we're being kept in this foetal position on the floor. The tension builds within me as my thoughts start to wander. What perversion will we face tonight? I wonder if the crazy guy who is paying for us is already in the room, watching. Maybe that's all he wants to do tonight. From what I've heard, less is more for some of these men.

Then I hear a whirring sound, a snap and…a cuckoo clock. *Coo-koo. Coo-koo.* I count them. Twelve times. It's midnight.

It's the last thing I expect. It's so comical that it's almost sinister. Especially when it's followed by another few minutes of utter quiet.

Something is happening now. The heavy door opens again, and I hear one set of footsteps. They seem to enter the room, and there's a dull shudder as I assume the door is closed again. The steps are lighter than the boot-like sounds I heard before — or maybe that's because there's only one person to hear. My senses are out of balance and maybe they're playing tricks on me. But I'm sure it's a man. It has that stride about it.

I'm intrigued.

The man's footsteps are the only sound now, and they are in no hurry. I hear them stop close behind me. There's a long pause. The waiting is unbearable. I'm ready to flinch at any moment, and I'm a nervous wreck. But no touch comes. He moves away to the right. I find myself trying to picture him.

What sort of man dreams up this kind of scene? Short, balding and ugly? But hang on — he must be decent-looking if he's a well-known figure. I start to think about British film stars, and that leads me to think about our mysterious and silent 'waker' from the school. I let my thoughts settle on the idea that it's him now walking around in front of me.

He's taking his time surveying us. Or is it only *me* he's surveying? Is his eye resting a little longer on Carla, or on Melissa? Is he touching *them*? It doesn't sound like it. The floorboards are about the only things that will speak to me here, but they're mute. What on earth is this all about?

He keeps pausing for a long time, taking a couple of steps, then pausing again. This feels like an inspection, plain and simple. Is he simply drinking us in, like Charles did on my first night in his service? Or is there more of a purpose to this? I'm getting antsy to know. This is an uncomfortable position to hold. Especially when you don't know what's coming.

Okay, now there's a little bit of movement. I can hear it loud and clear, away to my left. A floorboard creaks as I hear a transfer of weight. I hear the click of a bone somewhere, and a gentle thud. Then I hear a sharp intake of breath. It sounded feminine. Then it's quiet again — but I sense something is going on still. It lasts a good couple of minutes.

The action — whatever it is — comes closer to me now. To whoever the girl on my left is. I hear the floorboards again, a rustle of skin on carpet that hints at some kind of gentle movement. Then there's something like a tiny whimper from her. I would pay good money to tear off my blindfold and see what's happening. But clearly it's not the obvious thing. The sounds of that would be far less subtle.

What's *that* sound now? I can barely make it out, but it sounds like…pencil on paper. I would swear it's the noise of a determined writer, scrawling something. But why would he? Maybe it's some kind of tiny instrument instead. Oh God, I feel like I'm at the dentist. Waiting for a touch I don't know. My heart is going crazy. Whatever it is, it's coming close.

There's the unmistakeable sound of a man rising to his feet, and a deep sigh from my colleague next to me. I presume I'm next, and I wait with bated breath.

But nothing comes. The feet move directly past me, to what I am fairly sure is the other end of our row. I'm surprised and taken aback. I've been silly again, trying to anticipate too much. I'm a terrible gun-jumper sometimes.

My hair is in a pony-tail tonight, and I become aware of it slipping off my neck to the left. It grazes me and makes me realise just how sensitive my skin is right now. In spite of that little fear factor, I'm seriously turned on. Imperceptibly – I hope – I shake my head. I must have this mystery treatment. Whether I want to want it or not.

The sounds repeat away to my right. Once. Then again, closer. Oh…so he's leaving me for last. Or he's leaving me out completely.

Will this be like the chess game again? One big, long, drawn-out tease?

My tummy is tied in knots by the time he reaches me, lowers himself behind me and pulls my ankles roughly apart. I can't help gasping. My knees are next, and my kneecap thumps on the ground as I have to reposition one of them to widen my stance.

And now he's pushing the backs of my thighs, giving a clear signal that he wants my ass up in the air. His hands feel warm but rough. They push me into position like I'm a bendy doll. And now he stops manoeuvring me. My head is still down, my hands wrapped around it. He has me where he wants me. And I'm quivering.

Still there's no sound, although I can hear him breathing now, like a bear in no hurry, stalking in the knowledge that its prey will never win.

I'm shamefully aware that I'm on total, no-place-to-hide display. Like some kind of wild beast on heat, I'm on all-fours, my hind exposed for a worthy Alpha male. *Any* worthy Alpha male. My genitals are scarlet, inflamed, and parched for just one thing.

God, I'm burning and freezing at the same time. Shivering from my utter nakedness, yet perspiring from the wildfire ripping through me. I can feel the hair at my temples turning sticky with fear and need.

I'm flinching and twitching, even as not one finger is laid upon my body. My pony tail keeps on tickling, and my breath comes in short gasps, the air infused with rich carpet fibres, the odour of burning and the distant waft of wood varnish.

Now comes that light scraping sound again. The pencil. I swear it, something is being written. At length. My ears strain, and I wonder if that's the sealing and parting of lips I can hear. Is he mouthing words to himself as he writes? My sense of hearing, desperate to discover something, anything, is at full stretch to try and pick out words.

But I don't think there are any words. Nothing more than lip movements from his wet, thoughtful mouth. Oh, I know it's wet, because it sounds like water dripping in a cave when he does that murmuring thing. Saliva.

And I know it's thoughtful, because he's writing. You only write when you're thinking.

My toes curl as I kneel there, quivering, while he writes things down as if he's forgotten I'm here. Like my family doctor used to do. Or maybe it's a drawing. A sketch. Several sketches. One for each of us. Right down to every fold and petal, showing clear and bright between our buttocks.

Then, suddenly, comes a touch. I jump. How did he move so quietly? My ears are my world right now, yet I didn't hear his arms move. Oh, but...never mind that. Touch has just supplanted hearing in the pantheon of my senses. Touch, with two hands.

I can feel his thumbs far behind me, pulling me open, fingers splayed across each buttock. They rest like feathers, while the thumbs tug with the firmness of a harsh surgical tool.

I'm forgetting to breathe.

There's nothing to see. Only feel.

He stretches me wide apart at the top. Then in the middle. Then at the bottom. He holds me in each position for several seconds. I hold my breath.

Something is telling me to feel incensed. Part of me insists that I stand, tear off the blindfold, demand my clothes and call a taxi.

Yet my clit is whimpering for touch. And somehow I only hear that bud of mine.

She gets her answer as his thumbs move closer together at the raging delta of my pussy. My tail bone thrusts into the air, and I swear I hear a whispered chuckle. Just an air-fuelled snort of which I don't like the sound.

He pulls even harder now, no doubt teasing my hiding clit out into the open. He holds, and holds, and I'm so turned on I'm dying. So close, yet…

Now he does a deft thing with his hands, an acrobatic finger leaping right onto the spot. There it is. The whimper. The tiny groan. It's exactly the sound the other girls made. Now I understand.

It's fleeting. A second — long enough to gasp — and no more. It's a pure and perfect tease, one that has surely worked on all five of us. When his finger goes into me a moment later, it doesn't stay for very long. It's like absent-minded probing. An inspection, almost. Then he spreads my lips again, and my forehead reddens on the carpet as I think about how wet I must be right now. Oh, he can surely see that.

I am dying to rip off this blindfold once more, but this time it's only because I want to lay eyes on the mystery stranger with the strong, taunting fingers.

The thought that he is a pussy connoisseur takes hold of me and overwhelms me. It thrills me also.

He pulls my buttocks wide open from the centre, briefly making my anus gape. He holds and looks for some time, but doesn't intrude there. I am almost hurting from the need for a prolonged touch. Anywhere down there will do. Please.

But he lets go. And suddenly the silent one is breathing words in my ear. His voice is hot and potent from the closeness. It sounds like a thunderstorm when he speaks. And when the words come, that storm turns into a hurricane in my head.

"I know you, Emma Carling," it coos with threatening pleasure. Then, in a harsh, urgent whisper that blazes in my eardrum like cannonballs, "I've known you a very long time indeed."

VI

The moment I hear those words whispered, a howling worry takes me in its grip. Who the hell was that? Does he mean me harm? I must know. But I have been told I may say nothing; ask nothing.

Where a moment ago there was passion and longing curiosity, now there is fear. My itch to know who was touching me has been replaced by a desperate desire for information. Suddenly, I find myself in conditions of psychological torture.

This is someone who knows what I am doing with my life. It could be anybody. My secret could be out already. I feel my stomach flip as I realise that a malicious soul could have put my bare pussy on Facebook already. Twitter. Maybe both.

But no, wait a moment. Surely Lucy would never send us to someone who would do that? Privacy is one of her watchwords.

Still, she did seem unusually nervous earlier this evening.

Oh, Christ, I'm imagining the very word. Fuck, I need to look. I *have* to know. I'm burning sick with worry.

It doesn't help that the hot, softer-than-soft whisper appeared to be the climax of the evening for this man. Having left me till last, and murmured me a horror cliffhanger, he moves away and, judging from the way the shoes-on-wood sound fades out, leaves the room.

Then our exit process commences. It's like our arrival in reverse. A crew arrives to steer us out and dress us, with Esmeralda directing operations. The blindfold, of course, goes nowhere. We're led to what I assume is Lucy's car.

I'm so happy when the doors slam shut and it's *her* voice I can hear. She is always such a comfort.

"Have a nice time in there, ladies?" she asks once we're safely inside the vehicle.

The girls, though still blindfolded, are suddenly full of babble. Everyone wants to compare notes about the weird events of the evening. Lucy doesn't sound at all surprised when she's told there was no actual sex.

"It was kind of like we were being displayed, or, I dunno, examined or something!" Carla exclaims.

"Exactly!" yelps Teresa. "Hey, did anyone else hear that scratching sound? Like a pencil on paper?"

Murmurs of agreement fill the car.

Lucy chuckles as her Mercedes C-Class moves gently through the streets. "Well, girls, an inspection is pretty much exactly what that was."

There's another murmur, but I'm barely listening to her and haven't spoken a word. The growing distance between us and the place we've just been is doing nothing to ease my troubles. I daren't say anything about that demonic voice in my ear. Not yet, anyway. I need to think about this. And furious thinking makes me go quiet.

"You see," Lucy begins, "one or two of my big clients like to examine my latest talent in the same way they would select ripe apples at the greengrocer. It gives them some kind of imperial feeling. And a massive power trip.

"I suppose the selection process gives them something that simply hiring one of you — or all of you — for sex wouldn't. A lot of the gentlemen, you see, consider themselves connoisseurs of the female body. Like wine collectors, they enjoy the choosing and the tasting before they pick what's right for their cellar. That's as much a part of it as the drinking. Do you follow?"

"Makes some sense, I guess," says Melissa. "It doesn't change my feeling that men are weird though!"

There's laughter, but I don't join in. I'm silent, and looking out of the window. Or at least I would be if it wasn't for the blindfold. Which is really starting to get on my nerves. It's an irritant I seriously don't need right now.

"So we get a grand for not even having sex?" asks Teresa, a note of wonder in her voice. We haven't really spoken before, but I think it might be her very first assignment for Lucy.

"Correct, ladies," says our lovely agent. "And it's nothing to what you'll make if you're chosen as one of his favourites. Think of this as a kind of free trial. One that's well worth doing."

The thought that 'free' in my new line of employment can actually mean £1000 cheers me up just a little.

"So, the pencil…was he taking notes or something?" enquires Carla. "Is it just one guy? Can you say who it is?"

"He was indeed taking notes, I should imagine," Lucy replies. "Yes, it's just a single client in this case, and he —"

"It sounded like he had helpers though!" interrupts Carla.

"Naturally! Servants and assistants all add to the power sensation," Lucy resumes. "And no, I certainly can't say who it is unless he decides to reveal himself. Or gives me permission to speak his name. In this case, that won't be any time soon. If ever."

"So then, it would have to be a blindfold every time with this guy?" asks Teresa.

"More or less," says Lucy. "But there are other ways too. He could wear a mask. He could simply forbid you to turn around. He could have you in a dark room."

There's a pause.

"I know what you're all thinking," Lucy says. "Yes, it has the potential to be a pretty exciting gig. I'd be a little jealous…

"Anyway," she continues, snapping out of her rare display of wistfulness. "I'm sure I don't need to remind you girls that you need to have the utmost awareness of the need for guarding your clients' activities behind a curtain of privacy. In this respect it is much like doctor-patient confidentiality."

That makes me feel grumpy again. What about *my* confidentiality? *My* privacy?

"They wouldn't take photos, would they?" I pipe up suddenly.

Lucy snorts. "I'm rolling my eyes at you now, Emma Carling! Photos? What do you take me for? You know that every client contract forbids this. And they are told in no uncertain terms that if I find out there's been any attempt at taking pictures, then that's the last they'll have to do with me or any of my girls."

Yeah, I think to myself. I'm sure there are plenty of other Lucies and plenty of other girls in London. If someone had something personal against a girl…

"Is everything okay, Emma?" asks Lucy gently. "You were rather quiet until just now."

"I'm fine," I answer. I'm quite sure I don't want to go into it with her right now. "It was just a bit unsettling, with the blindfold and everything. I'll get used to it."

"I know you will," says Lucy. You could almost hear the smile in her voice.

I go back to shuddering gently as the spotlight moves away from me. I rack my brains. Who could he be? The voice itself is no help to me. It was so close, almost inside my very ear, that I wouldn't have known if it belonged to my dearest friend.

Potential names fly through my head. Exes. Former colleagues. Or one of my father's wealthier friends. It's certainly got to be someone who is loaded. That rules out most exes, I suppose. Except Peter Sawkins. I've been told he's come into some serious cash after some clever investments. Fuck, and it didn't exactly end well with him. *Would* he? He has a mean streak, but…could it go this far?

Colleagues? Wealthy ones? None of my recent peers qualify. But maybe a few former bosses do. My blood freezes as I picture the CEO of the firm I spectacularly walked out of last month. The very same one who lectured us at training.

Ah yes, and what *about* Cranleigh House? Rupert? Hmm, I think I might not mind if it were him. The waker guy, whose name I never did find out? Harry the Scotsman, whose cock I sucked in the sunshine by the pool, right in front of everyone? Chris the chauffeur? What a thought.

Well, at least the guys from training would be discrete, wouldn't they? They know the game. They work closely with the agencies. If it's one of them, they're surely just fucking with my mind, right? That would be typical of the bastards. But at least it would be safe.

If only I could know, I might get some sleep tonight. Listening to the chatter going on in the car, I figure nobody else is hung up on who the guy might be. It sounds like they all had more or less the same experience that I did, apart from that fatal whisper. Not one of the girls mentions a frightening murmur in her ear. That seems to have been reserved for the centrepiece. The girl who was saved for last. Yay, lucky me.

"God, how about that fingerwork?" says Carla. She's like another Alyssia: these Australian girls are shameless. "All that teasing and stretching, then just that perfect little touch on exactly the right spot. Ugh…and then nothing!"

"Yep, that sounds pretty familiar," chirps Melissa. "I'm pretty wound up after that. And there's something about a blindfold, isn't there?"

More murmurs of approval. I cast my mind back to how I felt before those chilling words were uttered to me. And in spite of myself, a tiny current of horniness ripples out from the core of my soul.

The dread is back again once Lucy drops me — last of the five — back at my flat. I'm relieved I can take the blindfold off before getting out of the car, but there's not much else to cheer me as I walk in the front door. I'm so concerned that I don't even think about pressing my vibrator into action. Normally, after that much of a sexual wind-up, it would be my first port of call.

I wonder if I should have said something to Lucy once we were alone in the car. I've always felt like I would be able to tell her anything, but all of a sudden I'm not so sure. Not because I don't think she'd look out for me. Precisely the opposite, in fact. If I suggest that a client has made me feel uncomfortable, she'd have to say something to them. And that, if the guy knows me and, God forbid, knows my family, could make things worse. I'm probably not thinking straight, but I'd rather play it cool.

I can't come up with any better plan than that as I toss and turn for most of the night. By sunrise I'm exhausted, unable to nod off, and I end up gazing at the skylight once more. As always, it calms me, especially since this morning's dawn is making a lovely mauve-orange light show above my head.

It's not so bad, I tell myself. I'll be getting another grand in the bank today. And the fact that such a figure is already starting to feel like pocket money makes me think that what will be, will be. I'm going to stick at this!

What's more, I've got nothing much planned for today. No clients and no appointments. Except for the long-overdue dinner with Martin in the evening. And tomorrow, I've got Sarah arriving. I allow myself a little smile.

I spend the day catching up on some reading, while grabbing the odd snack from the deli across the road. It's a strange feeling not to even look at the prices, but I'm starting to get used to just picking whatever takes my fancy. The Polish girl behind the counter knows my face now, and gives me a wide smile every time I go in. I've started tipping her. Why? Because she's sweet to me, and because all of a sudden I can afford to do it. Where my new lifestyle and career is concerned, I want everyone to be a winner.

Martin draws a short straw in the evening though, because I mess up most of the dinner I attempt to make for us. My cooking has always been hit-and-miss. Tonight, what sounded so straightforward in Jamie Oliver's book went badly wrong in Emma Carling's kitchen. I thought I was keeping it simple with vegetable linguine, but perhaps beans on toast is where I should draw the line.

Thankfully, I know Martin well enough to joke about it. "At least I can afford a cooking course now," I murmur apologetically. "Maybe an autumn retreat in Tuscany for a week. I should at least learn how to get pasta right, shouldn't I?"

Martin, who is a fine cook and has prepared me many a tasty meal in his kitchen, chuckles warmly. "Sounds like a lot of fun. But tonight's experiment doesn't matter, you know. It's the thought that counts. And the chance to catch up with *you*.

"And anyway," he goes on, reaching for another top-drawer bottle of Chianti, "we've got our second round of this delicious wine to finish!"

"We sure do," I grin, holding out my glass. "At least I couldn't cock that part up. I think we had to spit the wine out the last time I had you over, didn't we? My budget's a tiny bit healthier now…"

"And here's to that!" he booms as we clink glasses.

"Oh yes," I blurt out, blushing a little. "I should give you a huge thank you. I didn't ever imagine it could all work out, especially so fast. And I didn't seriously believe the money you mentioned when you first brought up the subject of, you know…"

"But now it's in your bank account," he chimes in. "And you're having fun, aren't you?"

He gives me a wink.

I redden a touch more: "Maybe a little. Anyway, thanks for steering me in this direction. It would never have crossed my mind, obviously. I'd probably be working in that coffee shop downstairs if it wasn't for you."

"Well, I would have hated to see that," he smiles. "I'm glad you're using your good looks and, ahem, your fine skills. Clearly the school taught you a few useful tricks."

"Hey, are you saying I was useless in bed before?" I ask in mock outrage.

"I'm sure you were useless just about everywhere," he replies drily. His wit almost makes me fall off my chair with laughter.

The evening flies by this way, full of banter, euphemism and innuendo. It's always been like that with Martin. I feel comfortable enough that I could tell him anything, but we choose to be just a little bit British about things nonetheless. As a platonic but dear friend, it feels better that way.

Of course, I do tell him how well his friend Charles treated me, and how amazing he made me feel. I also tell him it didn't feel much like an assignment.

"I'm sure it didn't," he nods. "Our Charles loves to make a woman feel special. That's his pleasure. It's just that he doesn't see why he should promise himself to one lady for life. And since women tend to get attached to him, he prefers the escort approach.

"I must say he's extremely taken with you though! Don't worry, he didn't share details, but I've never heard him rave about a girl quite like this. Who knows, maybe you can change him!

"I think I'll just stick to the day job for now," I grin. But I can totally see why women would get attached to Charles. I've got first-hand experience of that. I tell Martin a few other tidbits, and then I mention that strange whisper from last night. It hasn't bugged me so much today, but it's been on my mind.

Martin frowns as I tell him more or less — minus the naked fingering — what happened.

"I wish I knew what to say, Em," he says. "I'm no expert, and it's hard to guess whether it's really anything to worry about. I can understand why you don't want family and friends being told, although I think that with time you'll come to realise it's not such a big deal.

"It *could* just be someone messing with you. Any client knows your name is Emma, right?"

"Right, but Lucy's always said that they aren't told surnames…"

"I see. Although surnames aren't difficult to track down nowadays. But look, why don't you mention it to Lucy? She seems to have your best interests at heart. She's very experienced and I'm sure she would sort out any uncomfortable situation."

"I know, I know," I murmur thoughtfully. "I just think I want to know a little more first. I mean, maybe I don't make the cut with this client and the whole thing goes away…"

"It's unlikely you won't make his list," Martin responds, unashamedly looking me up and down, even though I'm in my oldest, grubbiest house tracksuit.

"Er, maybe so," I sigh uncomfortably. "I guess I'm just being stubborn, but I have this thing about fighting my own battles. When I got bullied at school and I told my brother about it…" I pause for a moment. "He chased them away, you know, but it was embarrassing. And they just had more ammunition on me the next time."

"I get you, darling," says Martin in his reassuring way. "I'm certain you'll do the right thing. Things will work out. Just look how far you've come."

I smile weakly at him, emotional from the alcohol and from our reunion. He's right: I've come miles and miles and miles. And things *do* seem to keep working out. I just hope that chilling whisper will get out of my head soon.

VII

I open the door, and Sarah almost knocks me over. She pulls me into a warm embrace and holds me tight. For what seems like ages, it feels like we're glued together. It's pretty nice. It's been over a month since we've been together, and I'm excited that she's here. I'm happy to have her hold me.

And then we're kissing. It just happens. And God, it's beautiful. The thing that I've been missing during this early part of my new career is suddenly so obvious. Locking lips with a girl is *real* kissing. It gives me something that none of my clients — nor any man ever — quite manage to deliver. A woman knows how a woman wants it.

And what's more, I've got an emotional bond with this person. Back at the school, she seduced me, the unwilling, virgin bisexual, plain and simple. And I can feel that special connection sparking again each time our tongues touch and intertwine, our love — is that going a bit far? — pouring into each other's mouths, then deep into our bodies. Deep as you can go.

Jesus, I'm turning to mush. I don't think I knew just how much I missed Sarah until now.

I hear a door click shut down the hallway. Hastily I pull away from Sarah, who seems to have been grinning like a Cheshire Cat even while kissing me. I glance down the hallway. Shit, it's Mrs Hampstead! A sweet, dear little old lady if ever there was one. She's probably never heard of…well, the kind of thing we were up to. And there she is, slowly turning away from her door and moving towards us.

But if she *did* spot the two young women kissing at the other end of the corridor, she's not letting on. I'm guessing she didn't see us, because I think she'd have stopped and stared if she had. For her, it would be like seeing a UFO.

"Hello Mrs Hampstead," I wave, hoping that pretending everything is normal will make her think she imagined anything she might have thought she saw.

"Good morning, young Emma," she smiles as she heads around the corner towards the elevator. "And to your friend!"

"Come on, friend," I wink at Sarah, "Get inside, will you? I don't want to be responsible for any heart attacks."

"Whatever," she says, picking up her bags and stumbling into my poky little flat, "You're just being shy again, you prude!"

"Hey!" I protest as I close the door behind her. "Just you wait until you hear some of the things I've been up to. No prudes here!"

"We'll see about that, Missy, but I definitely hope not!" she says hotly. "And I seriously hope the work sex hasn't tired you out too much for play sex."

I'm feeling a bit impish, so pause for a moment before saying, "Well, a little, actually. I've cleared you some room on the sofa. It should be just about long enough for—"

"Oh fuck off!" she squeals indignantly. And then I burst out laughing, and she drops her bag and grabs my arms again. "Don't even joke, baby. That would be the worst kind of torture. Now show me to your chamber, m'lady!"

I flutter my eyelashes playfully, then take her by the hand and bring her through. Of course I've prepared, really. In anticipation of her arrival I've already tidied up, lit some scented candles and cleared her some space in the wardrobe.

"It's going to be a squeeze, this room," I apologise sincerely. "But I'm thinking that—"

"As long as it's got you in it!" she interjects, breathing heavily.

Oh! I wasn't really thinking of immediate sex while I got set for Sarah's arrival. In fact, I wasn't really sure just who or what she was to me now that we're back in the real world. But now all those questions have disappeared into the lustful smoulder that hangs between us. And before I know it we're making love again.

I'm not sure that 'making love' is a phrase that's ever come naturally before, given the quality of my previous relationships. But there you go, it's just happened. Making love on the bed. On a Wednesday afternoon, while the sun streams in through my skylight. This is the life!

The love-making — hell, Sarah Smith turns the Emma Carling sex machine into pure goo! — is terrific. So fucking good, she makes my body shiver in incredible ways. I'd forgotten some of the things she can do, mostly with her tongue, and her lips, and her teeth. Yet always on the soft and tender side.

Doing it with a woman is just so different. It's been a missing piece in the puzzle of my life ever since training ended. I'm stunned how fast my life has changed. My sexual need has become a beast that needs constant feeding. And I must say, I'm really enjoying the mealtimes.

I indulge in a rare cigarette as we lie in bed for the rest of the day, enjoying not needing to be anywhere. We catch up on all the happenings of the past month or so. Not for the first time, I begin to get the uncomfortable feeling that I've had a far more interesting time than Sarah has. After a while, I cut short my debauched tales and listen to her.

"I've been thinking a lot since school," she says, "but not doing very much. I still had a month left on my lease in Brighton, so I've just been hanging around really. I guess I've been trying to convince myself to go back to drama school, but I just haven't felt my heart in it. Plus, I got my grades back, and they didn't fill me with encouragement. Let's just say I might not be very good at acting."

I do wish this lovely girl wouldn't switch into downcast mode so easily. For all I know she really *isn't* any good on stage, but I do know that she deserves to be happy. I have to stop myself asking if she has thought about going back to her family for a while when I remember, just in time, that her mum and dad both passed away in her teens. Sarah's life makes mine look like a bloody holiday camp, and I'm almost ashamed to have ever complained about anything. I just know I really want to help her.

"Okay," I murmur thoughtfully, "but we know you're very talented in the bedroom."

"Not sure those folks at Cranleigh House agree, though, did they? I mean, I passed, but, my report card…I don't know if I'm up to it…"

"Bollocks!" I say firmly. I'm feeling a bit of a personal mission coming on as I lie here beside my friend. I badly want Sarah to come and enjoy some of the life I've been enjoying for myself. "You've got every bit of skill *I've* got, maybe more, and I don't care what those teachers said. In fact, I'm pretty sure I'm not as good as they think I am."

She splutters. "You keep telling yourself that, Miss Modest!"

I really can't seem to get used to all this fanfare about my performance, or desirability, or whatever you call it. I just wasn't brought up to be able to handle it. But I'm constantly wondering if all this adulation has always been out there, just waiting for me to open the window and hear it.

"Never mind about me," I retort, trying to sound serious. "Do you want to be a highly paid prostitute with me or not?"

"It sounds ace to me, yes! I'm already running out of money, and the sex part sounds like *quite* a lot of fun.

There's a note in her voice that reminds me to ask her something that's been bugging me.

"I've been meaning to ask you," I begin, hoping to sound vaguely tactful. "Where do you really stand on men? I kind of get the impression you're more into girls. And most of the work, you know, is… you get my drift?"

She laughs raucously, as though she's doing some kind of voice projection exercise back at drama school. "Look, you're a little biased Miss Carling! Most of the work you've seen me do is somewhere between your legs."

At this I close my eyes and feel the corners of my mouth curling into a wistful smile. I can't help myself.

I feel her pull me a little closer as I do that, as if it's all the invitation she needs to demonstrate her skills again. I'm so tempted to let her hand roam, but I catch it just as she starts to slide her palm down across my belly button.

"Wait, don't change the subject!" I admonish.

"Right, sorry, okay, where was I? No, look, I'm bisexual. My first choice, I must admit, does tend to be women. Although at the moment it's just *one* woman."

She clears her throat and goes on: "But I do love cock as well, you really don't need to worry. That time that you and me did the double penetration at Cranleigh? It was special for being the first time we worked together, but trust me, Emma, I think about those two men inside me every single day."

"Well, good," I say, cheered by the news, and feeling momentarily like I've morphed into Miss Jackson, grading her for her open love of cock. "Then we should set about getting you paid to enjoy some *more* men inside you, shouldn't we? There's more than enough out there to go round."

Stupidly, I blush. She smiles, unconvincingly, her less confident side coming to the fore once again. "Why 'we'? You don't have to spend your time helping me out, you know!"

I give her a look. "Well, I want to, so take that!"

It seems wrong, after all, to just sit back on all this success while my best friend — or seemingly more than that — from school gets none of it. "We're in this together sister!"

Now she looks like she might cry. But then she smiles. I think she might be a tiny little bit unbalanced, our Sarah. "Well, I guess I *was* a little bit more pleasant to you than your little friend Petra...!"

"Oh God, I'd forgotten her! Now she can *definitely* fuck off."

"I wonder what she's up to?"

"Well, she didn't pass training, we know that. So if I understand rightly, no agent is likely to want her on their books. Not a serious agent anyway."

"Haha, hopefully for her sake Starbucks have got vacancies then!"

"Yikes, I wouldn't want her making my coffee. She'd probably spit in it. Anyway, stop changing the subject. Back to you!"

I squeeze her hand, which still rests on my stomach. It's supposed to show I'm serious about this conversation, but she doesn't take it that way. She pulls her knee in towards mine, draping it over my leg as I lie on my back, trying to keep my focus as I stare out of the skylight.

Sarah was among the few girls at training who didn't have a sponsor — and maybe the one girl who really needed one. She'd approached an agent in Brighton, who'd mentioned her to a London colleague, who then set everything up. But Sarah never ran into a Charles, and nor did that agent want to back her financially. So she'd had to foot the bill herself, scraping together pretty much every penny she had. And now she's got no easy path to work now that she's done.

"Haven't you at least spoken to the agent who put you in touch with the school?" I query.

"I did. They said I should come and see them when I'm in London. But they didn't sound all that excited. I think they must have seen my report."

"Hey, I'm sure it wasn't *that* bad! Bad would be failing, wouldn't it? And not everyone gets distinctions, you know. I'm not even sure Latifa got one, and look what a sexy devil she is! It certainly can't be essential for picking up good work, or there wouldn't be enough girls to serve London."

"Hmm, maybe. Well, I'll ring them tomorrow, I promise."

"Good. And meantime, I'll call Lucy and have a word. Maybe she values my opinion, and can do something for you."

She brightens. "That would be amazing Em! I don't even want to let myself think about how hot it would be to be working with you. To get paid for that kind of fun..."

I fear she's getting ahead of herself again, but at least she's on my page. Broadly speaking.

"And don't give a thought to money," I announce. "You'll stay here with me and I'll look after you. We'll have a whole lot of fun, and maybe we can get Latifa and Alyssia down for a weekend. We'll all go out!"

"You're the best," she grins. "And I'm sure I'll make it worth your while."

She winks at me. "Plus I'll wash the dishes."

"Haha, if you like! Although I want to move soon, and maybe get someone in to do that kind of work. Now there's something you can help me with. We're gonna go house-hunting! A bigger, better flat to suit my new income. What do you say? You can even have your own room!"

"Seriously, you better stop saying that," she grumbles. "You're stuck with me in your bed, like it or not."

"Like it," I whisper, satisfied that we've achieved some progress this afternoon.

And then her mouth is on my nipple. We don't hold ourselves back another moment longer.

VIII

*H*arley Street. This is where London's best doctors hang out. All the way down the road, gold plaques hang next to dull-coloured doors above the grey pavement. Every one of these physicians is a specialist in something very specific. And judging from the cars parked along the street, they're doing okay for themselves.

My heart beats a little quicker as my eye falls on the gold plaque in front of me. *Dr D.K. Krasznik, PhD.* Lots of other abbreviations I don't understand follow his name.

I've grown accustomed to my weekly sexual health check-up. A sweet lady doctor near my home takes care of that, and we have a good chat while she does her thing to make sure I'm safe. It makes me comfortable, and I've forgotten the shyness that overcame me in my first couple of appointments.

But I'm not feeling so good about this particular doctor's visit. This man is a pain specialist. A special kind of pain specialist.

I'm so glad I didn't meet anyone I know as I walked here and pushed the big white doorbell button. They'd be surprised to see me here, because everyone knows I've never had any health trouble.

Hopefully, they'd have been too polite to ask. But you couldn't bank on that with some of my nosey aunts.

I'd have had to lie, I muse, praying that the door will open quickly. Because the truth is there's nothing wrong with me at all. Although you might say I'm insane to be presenting my body to this man.

It's not a prostitution assignment. This is one of Lucy's screening things. This Dr Krasznik's job is to establish where my pain threshold is. It's supposed to be for my own good, but nothing about it sounds like fun. I feel distinctly nervous as a male voice on the intercom tells me to push the door open and proceed to the end of the hallway.

A buzzer sounds and I do as instructed. When I reach the end of the dimly lit corridor, a door opens and a man — Dr K I presume — ushers me into his office in business-like fashion. He gives me no more than a nod, and straight away I get the impression he's not worried about repeat business.

He motions me to sit on that little bed thing doctors always have in the corner of their room (although his room is a big one). I don't feel much like talking, so I sit upright and scrutinise him. He's in his forties, has unkempt black hair, and carries a trimmed beard with just a few grey hairs poking through. Beneath his white doctor's coat, I can see he's wearing a grey shirt and a red tie. The red in particular contrasts loudly with his sharp, serious features and his cool manner.

A portly nurse looks on as he prepares for my examination. I didn't notice her at first, and her presence doesn't make me feel any easier. She doesn't smile. Krasznik has hardly had a word to say to me since I arrived, and I get the impression this kind of appointment is totally routine for him. I wonder how many doctors specialise in this sort of thing? I imagine he gets paid a lot, working on Harley Street and all that.

Then again, so do I. And it was Lucy who sent me here, so it's all going to be fine. I don't like these people, but I tell myself to man up. So to speak.

"Are you hungry, thirsty or in need of the toilet?" Krasznik asks, looking me straight in the eyes for just about the first time today. They're very dark, his eyes. You can barely even make out the pupils. You certainly can't see anything resembling feeling.

I gulp. Then I remember to shake my head. I simply can't shake the nerves, and my pulse is racing hard. My legs sway nervously as they dangle over the side of the table. It's uncomfortable and functional, the bed thing. A bit like this whole experience.

"Then we will begin," he announces in an even tone, holding out a hand to his assistant. She hands him what looks like a giant pair of tweezers. It's the sort of thing my father would use to turn meat on the barbecue, on those rare occasions when we would have decent weather on holiday in Yorkshire.

"Unbutton your blouse," he commands.

His authority is impressive. It overpowers his rudeness and unpleasantness. I do exactly as he instructs, button by button. Quickly my blouse unfurls.

He surveys my plain white bra with cold disinterest. Well, I didn't feel like wasting my classy new stuff on this particular outing when I dressed this morning. So I'm wearing a bit of a throwback. Something decidedly comfortable. A relic from the days before Guia La Bruna came into my life.

"I will need your breasts to be bare, please," he says with a strange mix of patience and impatience.

Fine. He only had to ask. I don't think that whole 'initiative' thing Miss Jackson kept going on about is something I'm going to feel like switching on today. This man gets my back up. I reach behind me and flick open the clasp between my shoulder blades. The bra drops into my lap.

I get a flash of nostalgia about how easy this type of underwear is.

And then I remember that I need to be brave. Resistance isn't going to make this encounter with the tweezers any easier. So I take a deep breath and lean back on my hands, my blouse hanging open and my tits waiting for whatever he has planned. Behind them, though, my heart beats like a throaty drum.

I don't much like his eyes or his manner, and resolve to stay as stoic as I would if I were getting jabbed with an inoculation needle. No eye contact. Think about something else. *Anything* else.

He takes a step forward and applies the tong to my left nipple, holding my right shoulder steady with his hand. Not in a reassuring way. It's for steadiness. No more. No less.

It's only a gentle squeeze at first. I don't feel the need to move or say anything. All I notice is my stomach muscles and my thigh muscles tightening. Without my say-so. And I wonder what the large nurse is thinking about all of this. Because this sure as hell isn't the kind of nursing they teach you in training, I think to myself.

I wonder if she's jealous. She's not very attractive. I suspect she's single, and nobody is lining up to stimulate *her* nipples.

My strange musing snaps as Krasznik squeezes a little harder.

Then my thoughts go back to the nurse's training. Training…ah yes! She must have trained for her vocation. Just as I trained for mine. Very different training, to be sure. And yet here we are on a Thursday morning, each of us — in our own way — going about the work we trained for.

It's funny, the different things women can do in life. But I'm guessing she can't earn four figures in a couple of hours.

Ow! I snap out of my smug daydream once more as he gives my nipple a twist. I wince, suddenly consumed by what has become more than just a pleasant tickle of pain. And I can tell he's watching my reaction, so I close my eyes.

"Remember to breathe," he advises. Which seems sound enough counsel. My hurting breast rises and falls as I inhale and exhale deeply. I feel the searing sensation less on the exhale, but that's the moment he chooses to twist harder, adding a notch of power to the squeeze as he does it.

It's savage now. I yelp.

He's got the metal teeth where I imagine it hurts the most: halfway up my lengthening nipple. Not gripping the tip, but not resting against the areola either. Fuck, this guy had better know what he's doing.

"J...ff..." I begin, wanting to curse out loud. But I stop, because I don't want to give him the satisfaction. There's no right or wrong today, Lucy said. Wherever my limit is, is fine. But a strange pride in me — not a purely professional one — won't let me give in just yet.

God, I've got a nasty feeling I might be competitive about this. Like, I want to be the toughest escort in London. Emma Carling can take anything, they'll say. She's your girl, Lucy will tell her kinkiest clients.

Crumbs, why do I want *that*? My roasting nipples are screaming at me not to want that. And now he starts to pull. Just dead straight. A pure tug that stretches my poor left breast into a weird conical shape, all the while maintaining the twist and squeeze.

It's...oh, God, it's...quite pleasant. Even though it hurts like fuck knows what. Even though I hate the guy.

I notice that my right nipple — the one that hasn't been touched — is standing to attention.

My own attention jerks back to the left as he twists it all the way in the other direction, ramping up the squeeze even more. This time I *do* curse, and loudly. He seems to have been expecting the foul-mouthed reaction. He lets go. My breast shivers back into its normal position.

I notice how blood-red it has gone, and none of us says a word.

The weird and exhausting appointment goes on for another intense, never-ending hour. After his initial test by hand, Krasznik begins to get more scientific. He attaches sensors and electrodes to various parts of my body as he stimulates them using mechanical devices.

He keeps his words to a minimum, mostly just to instruct me to remove various items of clothing. Inevitably, I suppose, he spends a long time on my buttocks. One machine is set up to strike me lightly there, its mechanical arm fitted with something like a hairbrush with sharp spikes. All the while, those little sticky patches are taking measurements.

Another machine, which I somehow didn't see when I came in, thrashes me with a heavy cane until I cry. He sits impassively in front of me, writing on his clipboard and — I think — making a recording of my wailing responses.

Then he nods at the nurse to switch it off, after which she rubs something soothing into my skin.

But he's not done with my ass. He proceeds — I presume — to try my hole out for size. I've neither asked nor been asked for anal since Cranleigh House, and it feels weird once again as he invades me with a succession of lubricated butt plugs.

Never once does he ask me how I'm feeling. But he seems to know just when to stop. I'll give him that much. I watch as he hands the last anal plug to the nurse, and I'm amazed at the size of what I've just taken. It's certainly bigger than any male appendage I've ever seen. Wow.

My clit gets a mechanical squeezing too. I didn't know they made clips for clits. He watches me quietly as he turns a dial and the pinch gets harder. This really does something to me. I'm lying on the table with my legs open, doing my level best not to think sexy thoughts. It's good practice, actually, but I'm relieved when he turns off the painful pleasure.

Finally, he checks my breathing and my pulse — but only after a few minutes with a ball gag in my mouth. I'm a first-timer with one of those too, and I can't say it's all that comfortable. But then, I suppose that's the point.

At last it's time to get dressed and leave.

"We will send your reports to you by post," he says curtly, as if he's just valued a property or something.

I don't know what else there is to say. I don't feel as though 'thank you' is appropriate, and I strongly suspect this isn't the kind of doctor who gives you sweets, so all I say is "Okay," nod at the nurse and walk out of the door. She didn't say a word the whole time either, and I wonder if every day is like this for her.

I want to say I hated the whole thing. Mostly, I did. I'm certainly glad Lucy has assured me I won't ever have to undergo a doctor's visit quite like that again. I walk out feeling sore and violated. But, undeniably, a tiny part of me is also aroused.

I wince as I lower myself into the hard wooden chair at the coffee shop where I meet Lucy later that day. Really, I should have thought the venue through when we planned this. We could have gone to the place with the sofas!

"Yee-owtch," I squeak, looking at her with a watery smile.

She chuckles: "That good, huh?"

"It wasn't exactly sexy, if that's what you mean…" I clear my throat. "Although I suppose…with the right…you know…it might be…"

"It will indeed," smiles Lucy. "I can guarantee you that. But I'm sorry you had to go through that today. I still promise it's a one-off. It's for your own ultimate safety."

I nod. It's even hurting to lean forward and take a sip of my cappuccino. It feels like there is a gaping hole down there, while tiny devils with pitchforks dance all around it. My nipples haven't entirely recovered from their various ordeals yet either. If I'd known it would be like this, I wouldn't have arranged to meet Lucy straight after seeing Dr Krasznik.

"In a couple of weeks we'll have your results," she says, "and then I'll know which of the more extreme clients I can send you to while keeping you safe.

"There's big money in the kinky stuff, Emma. However, I will not allow you to be pushed further than you can handle. My gentlemen and I discuss limits in great detail, and I will *personally*—" she looks me square in the eye and tightens her knuckles around an ashtray for emphasis, "I will *personally* break the balls of any one of them who goes an inch beyond those limits with any of my girls."

At times like this, I question the sanity of not telling Lucy about the threatening words I heard at the blindfold house. It's comforting, as always, to have somebody so obviously and completely on my side. When I'm with Lucy it seems inconceivable that anything unpleasant could happen. Yet still something holds me back from recounting every detail from the 'inspection night' with the other girls.

Right now, though, I'm feeling a terrific urge to lie down, maybe with a little TLC from Sarah. So I resolve to get right to the point of why we're here.

"So, did you ever read the report on my friend Sarah?" I begin. "An English girl I was with at Cranleigh?"

"I read all the reports," grins Lucy. "It's my job to see what talent is out there. And after all, there are only about forty graduates each year. It's not much work."

I'm momentarily thrown. "Aren't there any other schools like that?" I ask, feeling a little dumb.

"Oh, I should say not! It's a one-of-a-kind, that place. Not even America has an escort training institution. You'd never guess that the one school like that, anywhere in the world, is in stuffy old England, would you?"

We're both amused as she points out this big, secret exception to English prudishness. But I'm conscious that we're straying off topic.

"No, I guess not. Anyway, so what did you think of Sarah?"

"I just know that nobody stood out quite like you did. I was happy that my intuitions were right. There's usually one young lady who seems made for this life, and it was abundantly clear from your report that you were the pick of this summer's bunch."

"But…you didn't think about giving a job to anyone else?"

She pauses before answering.

"Not much, no. I had a special interest in you, of course, since I helped enrol you. And for me, this is a quality game, not a quantity game. True quality is rare. That's why I only have a dozen or so girls on my books."

"I just thought, you know…" I feel awkward, and actually I'm not sure what I think. "Because Sarah seemed pretty talented to me. And she's just come down to London, and she's looking for work. She got blown off by the agency that enrolled her when she went to see them yesterday and…I just think she deserves a decent chance."

"Hmm, you know I have to be extremely selective, don't you, Emma? Harsh, even. If anyone else's report caught my eye it was that of young Latifa, and maybe her friend Alyssia. But they're not in London."

She's avoiding the subject of Sarah. I try to steer her back. "I think Sarah is underrated," I say with more conviction than I feel. "She's especially good with the ladies. I mean she's naturally passionate and…we have real chemistry."

That was my trump card. Maybe I can sell Sarah on her potential as a double act with me.

"I'm aware," Lucy smiles. "I heard of your excellent performance together at school. I know you're close. But there's a chance your judgement is a *little* biased."

I frown, in what I hope is a light-hearted way.

"But look," she says brightly. "I'm going to consider what you've said. I'll take a closer read of her report, and have a little think about your friend Sarah, okay?"

My frown turns to a smile. My work here is done for now.

IX

*R*est and skin cream do wonders for my war wounds. Sarah, of course, is only too happy to rub soothing gels into my skin. God, I love her! Long showers help me as well, although I wish I had a bath in my apartment. One of those is going to be absolute priority in my new place.

I love the fact that this job allows me so much R&R time. If only I had discovered this life sooner! I curse all those thousands of hours I sat in an office cubicle. Every vaguely pretty girl should do this — leave the offices to the men!

On second thoughts, I guess, too much competition wouldn't be so good for our earnings as prostitutes. It's a moot point anyway. I know ninety-nine out of a hundred girls would be too shy, guilt-laden and repressed to do what I'm doing.

Yes, it feels amazing to be a high-brow escort. But part of me still feels bad that Sarah's not getting a chance to have that life. I've started trying to help her with that, though, as well as make an effort not to beat myself up about it.

Within a few days, I'm all recovered from Dr Krasznik's intrusions, and I'm raring to go for my next assignment. Sarah inspects my naked body and assures me that there's no longer any sign of Dr K's handiwork. "You're good to go, Carling," she announces. "I'll hold the fort while you're out tonight."

Again I try not to feel bad, and want to change the subject. The subject being that I'm going off to have sex for giant bucks — £2500 for two hours in tonight's case — while she has to sit at home and watch crap TV.

I put my arm around her and tell her I can't wait till we head off on our first assignment together. She forces a smile back at me, and just then my buzzer rings. That'll be the chauffeur.

I'm starting to get used to this, especially as the drivers are tactful and professional enough not to try and make awkward chatter about where I'm going and what I'm doing. I'd absolutely hate that. I could easily buy a car of my own, I know, but I don't see a lot of point at the moment. Driving in the city is stressful and there's nowhere to park.

Twenty minutes later, I'm gliding through the revolving doors at the Imperial Grand Hotel in Kensington. It's a windy night with a bit of a chill; summer's losing its grip on London already. So I don't stop to admire the postcard location. It's just along the road from the Albert Memorial, and a couple of doors along from the Albert Hall.

Inside, it's all old-world charm. A broad, carpeted staircase rises up in front of me, a gold-glowing chandelier hanging above it. And it's flanked by varnished wooden banisters. I step into the marble-floor lobby, and notice small, old-fashioned elevators (the kind I wouldn't trust) tucked into the corridor around the side. It's all understated exclusivity rather than modern bells and whistles. I think the place only has about thirty rooms. And in a location like this, well, I dread to think what a room costs.

A smiling concierge nods at me. It's my first proper hotel visit, and Lucy has explained to me that I'll never be asked awkward questions by the staff. They'll know, but they'll hush. All I've got to do is leave my coat at the concierge desk and head straight up to room twenty-seven.

So the people working here must know *exactly* what I'm up to. I know *I'd* be gossiping about me if I worked in this hotel. My innocence in these matters has drained away like rushing bathwater. And although I'm worried one of my less successful school mates might be working reception at one of these places, I know the possibility goes with the territory. I understand that a lot of our work will happen in expensive hotels in the West End, Mayfair or the Square Mile, and there's no way it could go on without the quiet acquiescence of staff and management.

Part of me finds it kind of thrilling to be a part of this unspoken system. It's like an underworld that suburban people don't even think about. The kind of thing they think belongs only in the movies.

I'd have been so nervous about this a couple of weeks back. I'd have wanted to bolt. But now that I'm on my sixth or seventh assignment, I'm so much more confident that I have real business being here. I belong.

So I dump my coat, suddenly feeling highly exposed in the requested sapphire blue dress, which is high on both cleavage and hem line. I make my way in what I hope is dignified fashion to the foot of the stairs. Sure, my heart's beating like a hummingbird's wings, but I feel like I know what I'm doing. As I begin to climb, I glance across at the long relaxation area to my left.

It's a wide U-shape, with the lounge wrapping itself around the wooden bar, stocked with bountiful (and doubtless disgusting) bottles of brownish hue. Probably whisky, I should imagine. They do look like expensive tipples, though, and so does the barman. Well, I mean, his waist coat and *cravate* are tailored and polished…put it that way.

He's decanting something from a weird-shaped kind of vase into a flat glass crammed with ice. Probably some sophisticated whisky serving thing these show-offs feel they must have. I'll never buy into their shallow world, that's for sure. The barman slides the drink across the bar counter with a look into which I can read nothing.

The recipient of the drink has his back to me, but appears to be on the elderly side. He's sitting alone, and he gives the bar tender a nod as he takes his drink and mulls over it. There's nothing particularly fascinating about anything in the mildly populated lounge, and I'm about to keep climbing when I see something that I can't believe.

A skinny blonde, her back to me, materialises from somewhere beneath the staircase. The skinny blonde walks up to the older man who just received the whisky.

I can't see her face, but there's something powerfully familiar about the way she moves.

I take a second to process her. Then I know.

It's fucking Petra.

She turns her face towards the man, chin resting poutishly on her fingers, and I'm sure of it. Even from twenty yards away, I can spot the unmistakeable brand of mercenary chill that radiates from her eyes.

I climb a couple more stairs so that she won't turn around and find herself staring straight at Emma Carling. I really don't fancy a chat with her — ever. I can still see what's going on through the wedge between the banister and the ground-floor ceiling. She has no idea her room-mate from school is watching her in action.

And what I assume she's doing is touting for clients. Everyone told me that no agency would touch her after her school report. She's got to be working as what Lucy calls a 'hotel lobby whore'. So much for Starbucks, I think to myself. Petra has clearly decided she can still get business on her own.

I know I shouldn't be staring. And that I have somewhere exciting to be. But I'm struck dumb by the co-incidence. I suppose I shouldn't be completely surprised to find her kind in a place like this. But I want so badly to believe that even a street corner is too good for her.

Is that mean? Well, firstly, she's a bitch. And second, why would anyone pay high-class rates for someone so…mechanical? She hasn't smiled at the guy once since I've been watching her. God, she'll never learn. I mean, I've never done this lobby touting thing, but even I can see she's not much of a saleswoman.

I shake my head and smile to myself. I would hate to do what she's having to do, of course I would. She's got no Lucy, no support. And I bet she can't earn anywhere near as well. Having an agent gives you kudos, and gives clients an assurance of safety and discretion. Petra's on her own, working hard for her business. God knows how many hours she'll have to invest in this lobby. She might not get any takers at all.

Then again, she's still insanely attractive. Even from this distance, I envy the glow of her skin. That's the one thing she's got going for her. But still, it doesn't look like she's making much headway with this gentleman. He doesn't really seem to be giving her the time of day, much less falling for her amateurish attempts at fake charm.

And I hope that she'll have to walk away. Again and again and again. She's fucking getting just what she deserves. And until she turns into a human being, I won't change my mind on that.

Chuckling softly at the back of my throat, I decide to leave her to it. But not before snapping a cheeky shot on my mobile. It's unprofessional, I'm sure, but it's too good to miss. I can't wait to text it to Alyssia and Latifa when I get home. And I can't wait to show Sarah.

Then I leave the cold bitch to it. I march on up the stairs, feeling better about myself than ever. But a few nerves begin to jangle as I find the corridor for Room 27.

I'm told there's to be a Frenchman, Louis, waiting for me there. But a silly fear that there might have been a mistake with the room number gnaws at me. What if some respectable couple open the door? What if somebody I know opens the door? God, how the heck would I explain what I'm doing knocking on hotel room doors dressed like this? It doesn't bear thinking about.

But no, I've got it right. It's clear that the man who opens the door of Room 27 is expecting me. He's wearing only one of the hotel's luxuriant white bathrobes, an unlit cigarette hanging loosely from the side of his mouth. His slicked-back hair and sharp features are beguiling, and he's surprisingly young for what I take to be a typical client in this game. I'd put him at around thirty.

He says nothing as he opens the door. Instead, his dark eyes explore me. They travel all the way down my body to the pointy toe of my shoes, then all the way back up again. I'm standing in full view of what is thankfully an empty hallway, and I wish he'd invite me in before Petra or anyone else comes haring around the corner.

But I forget all about Petra, and the rest of the world, when his eyes finish their slow journey down and up my figure. They lock onto mine, and he gives me the most wicked smile I've ever seen on a man. The cigarette dangles effortlessly as he does so, and the whole thing makes me melt.

"Come in, Miss Carling," he purrs. His 'Miss' sounds like 'Meece' and the way he gurgles the 'r' in my surname couldn't be more French. I don't remember much French, but the sounds he's making bring my hot French teacher, Mr Beauchamp, back to my mind's eye. For a moment I'm right back in my classroom, feeling the dance in my stomach all over again.

He is just so impossibly French. He is in absolutely no hurry. He motions me to sit down on one of the two armchairs in the room, angled either side of a small coffee table. I accept his offer of a cognac, and then he asks me lots of questions about my life. Almost every time I answer, his eyes undress me. It's very distracting. In a thoroughly enjoyable way.

I'm never quite sure how much I should lead the conversation with a client, but I'm getting used to it. He seems happy to ask most of the questions, but I feel I need to show an interest too. I'm really fascinated that he even needs me here. He's both charming and good-looking. And he must be well-off to be staying in this hotel.

Although he's Parisian, he spends a lot of time here in London. As far as I can make out, he's a professional playboy of sorts. He speaks of reading, of going to shows, of visiting artists. There's no mention of work, and I can only imagine he's from some rich family. I think about biting him just to see if he has blue blood.

He tells me that he 'adored' the nude photos of me Lucy showed him. "I had to have you, Miss Carling," he says, every word driving me wild. It's an understated French accent, really. His English is perfect and he's educated enough to pronounce the 'h' in 'had'. But he does it with a hint of foreign harshness. And then there are those 'r's, which roll like soft, distant thunder, and those long, drawn-out vowels that seem to drip with possibility while you wait for them to end.

I already know that my main job tonight will be to fellate Louis. After we've sunk a couple of glasses of cognac I'm startled to notice that he's growing through the parting in his bathrobe. Instinctively I look away as the fleshy apparition catches the corner of my eye and my heart jumps into my mouth.

When my eyes return to meet his, he looks amused. "You are a prostitute, no?"

I blush, look down and nod. "Yes," I answer him, trying to sound firm.

"Then you will not be embarrassed, *non?*"

"No, Sir," I smile. And I look down at his ever-lengthening tip as it emerges further and further between the cotton hems.

"I like how you English girls are always so polite. As if you are guilty. It is different from back home."

The comment fires me up. Suddenly I want to show him I can be as proudly filthy as any Parisian tart. Without being asked, I sink down in front of him on my knees, fully dressed in the gorgeous sapphire dress and high heels.

He makes no objection as I run my hands up his bare calves and below the garment. They travel up his thighs and then I pull the robe open, the loose belt offering no resistance. I wriggle forward and immediately wrap my mouth around his still-hardening cock.

I think he really has just come straight from the shower. It tastes wonderful: clean, but with just a hint of eau de cologne about it. I cup his balls in my hand, remembering my lessons, and massage them gently, while at the same time letting my head bob up and down on his shaft.

I really do believe I could do this all night. There's nothing I'd rather do and nowhere I'd rather be. Before training, I was a little bit uncertain about the appeal of giving a blow-job; now you'd have to tear me away. Every so often, I look up to meet his eyes or read the pleasure on his face. It makes me tingle each time.

Another moment from training comes into my mind as he finally tightens and spurts his hot seed into my mouth. I'm ready for it and I gobble it all down, licking his waxed balls and shaft for several minutes afterwards. It's a wicked privilege to explore a man like this — and it's my living!

I smile to myself as Petra comes into my mind. I rather hope she's still working the lobby without any success.

Louis barely goes soft at all. Certainly not for long at any rate. Soon it's a fully erect cock banging the back of my throat once again. But this time he stands up and grips me by the hair. *God, he's going to mouth-fuck me.*

Lucy told me this was one of his favourite things. I brace myself. I know I can take it. His swelling is relentless as he begins to pound and my jaw starts to hurt. I am struggling for breath and beginning to drool: he shows no let-up. And my God, it's a turn-on.

"Drop your hands," he orders.

I've been using them to grip his legs and keep my balance, but I guess he wants me to rock. My palms fall onto my thighs and suddenly I find the fingers of my right hand travelling further south, reaching for my clit while I ride this violent wave.

I don't know what Miss Jackson's view on this would be, but she always said a client wants to see a girl really enjoying herself. In any case, Louis makes no objection to me touching myself. And I need it desperately, because every thrust of his thick flesh into my mouth is driving me wild.

His grunts tell me he's about to unleash again, and that thought is enough to take me over the edge too. My clit and his cock let go at exactly the same moment, and I simply have to grab his leg with my left hand again. I'm shuddering too much to keep still.

I close my eyes as he twitches and slows in my mouth and my orgasm makes my head spin. What an utterly amazing way to come! I just can't wait to discover more sex acts I'd never thought of until this adventure began.

I feel strangely European as I sit down with him for another cognac after it's all over. I'm still dressed as I was when I arrived, though my hair and lip gloss is a mess. I'm thankful for the brush and makeup kit in my handbag, one of the things on the essential checklist Lucy's given me for every assignment. After all, I need to go through that lobby once again.

I kiss Louis on the lips before I leave. I hope I'll be back, and suspect that I will be. We've probably gone overtime again. It keeps happening, and I keep not caring. And I'm in even less hurry at this particular hotel, because I don't much want to run into Petra.

But when I eventually do make it back downstairs to grab my coat from the concierge and scurry out of the front door, I do indeed spy the slight blonde as I peep beneath the railing once more. She's still hanging around in the bar. Right now she's got nobody to talk to, and is fiddling about on her phone. I've seen enough, and hastily turn my head before she spots me as I emerge into the foyer.

I can't deny the satisfaction at seeing her struggling for business while I've been doing my work with such passion upstairs. Maybe there's some justice in the world after all, I think to myself.

X

*A*s the next couple of weeks slip by and September becomes October, I feel pretty bloody fantastic about myself. Winter is closing in, and I think how bad things might be if I hadn't been whimsical enough to accept the offer of attending escort school. An offer which reviled me at first.

I'm pretty sure I'd be mildly depressed if I'd stuck to traditional job-hunting. Being broke and the lengthening of the darkness hours would have made me a miserable girl. I almost certainly wouldn't have found work yet, since everything I'm hearing suggests the economy has still to hit rock bottom. For just about everyone I know, life in London has a gloomy and desperate air about it these days.

But there's no seasonal misery for me now. Not *this* version of me. It tickles me that I've found such a creative, unusual way of turning my life around. It makes me feel clever and brave, because I've done something other girls in my circle wouldn't seriously consider. I feel like I'm being rewarded tenfold for taking that risk.

Okay, I'm not quite ready to talk about it, but I'm enjoying keeping people guessing now. Especially the former colleagues I'm still in touch with. In fact, it's even a little arousing when the male ones helpfully send me the occasional link to a suitable job they've spotted. When that happens I think about the innocent work they picture me doing. Desk, laptop, business blouse.

Heels, stockings…

If only they knew.

I smile inside my head every time I imagine their faces if I told them that I already have another job, and then tell them what it is. Being the new Emma Carling makes me feel nothing but sexy and powerful on the inside. Outside is another matter, but keeping it secret is fun. For now at least.

I'm uncomfortably aware that sooner or later I'm either going to have to tell a few people the truth or spin a convincing yarn. I'm not keen on either, so for now I'm content to make do with shrugs and smiles to bat away worried friends.

My diary has begun to fill fast. I'm seeing about eight men a week now, and I'm loving every minute of it. Lucy won't allow me more than two clients a day. 'A man paying your kind of fee deserves to have you horny and hungry, don't you think?'

As bloody usual, she's right.

We're still waiting for the results of my 'pain test' with the objectionable Dr Krasznik, so I haven't been assigned to anything involving more than a light spanking. I'm nervously awaiting the day when I'm asked to mete out some punishment of my own, but I think Lucy is still easing me in. I've worked alone, apart from one lesbian show — the guy didn't even touch us! — I performed with the gorgeous American Tracy. And I haven't had to deal with a man I find truly ugly yet.

On the whole, everything is going swimmingly. And I was much more comfortable when I saw Charles for the second time, about a month after my jittery debut night. Maybe it's because he treats me like a princess, but he's turning into an absolute favourite of mine. It was with a blush that I admitted to Lucy that I put in some substantial overtime with him the next morning. How could I say no to what he was doing to my nipples?

And when I eventually had to go, he insisted on paying me for my extra hours. I waved the offer away, blushing louder than ever as I told him it was entirely my choice. But when I got home, I found a wad of £50 notes in my handbag. He must have slipped them in there when I went to the bathroom.

No question, I am the luckiest girl in London. The cash keeps on rolling in, and before long my bank account has swollen into five figures. It's quite astonishing, and I feel giddy when I see the numbers on the screen at the ATM. I realise that even without a special effort to save, it'll likely be six figures by springtime.

Naturally enough, I guess, I am becoming more intrigued by the history of this amazing profession. Everything seems so good, the most fascinating thing for me is why more women don't take this fun, easy and lucrative path in life. I feel like I've totally misjudged men, sex and the world for most of my existence, and I've only just had my eyes opened. I want to learn more, so I use my ample spare time to do some reading.

I tuck into a book about prostitution in Ancient Greece. I can barely put it down, and my jaw drops when I discover that the Athenians had a system of state-run brothels. For them, marriage was a social and economic formality, and nobody pretended otherwise. Men were expected to seek their pleasures at the whorehouses, where the government of Solon employed women just like any other civil servants.

You can say what you like, but these people were certainly honest with themselves. I think hard about how my new way of life got driven to underground status, and whether we'd ever have a system like that in the western world ever again. I chuckle as I imagine a parliamentary debate about the subject: political correctness and aghast feminists would never let it get that far.

To my mind, though, the Greeks might have been onto something. Maybe there was less denial in their assessment of human nature than we have to live with today. Who exactly decided we were monogamous animals? As long as nobody is forced or trafficked into the kind of work I'm doing, then why shouldn't it be considered noble and good?

I keep reading, and discover that (as you'd expect) the state brothels were considered rather drab, and ditto their inmates. Athenian men who could afford better would 'go private', as it were, and frequent *hetairai*, who were something like a Greek answer to the Japanese *geisha*. While sexually talented and of course beautiful, these educated women provided quality conversation, companionship, dancing and music too. I imagine, a little smugly, that I'd have been one of those.

Then I read the memoirs of the mysterious Madame Claude, the most famous procuress of modern times. I discover that this astute and occasionally ruthless French businesswoman had 'looked after' some of the most famous names of the 20th century including — allegedly — John F Kennedy, Gianni Agnelli and assorted Middle Eastern royalty. I read about her fussy naked inspections, the education her girls were obliged to acquire, and the way she ruled herself out of prostituting herself because she didn't enjoy sex enough. Wow: so many echoes of my own very recent schooling. And again, it makes me feel like I've cracked the elite.

I love Madame Claude's most famous quote: 'There are two things people will always pay for: food and sex. And I was never destined to be a chef.' I wonder if I could be like Madame Claude, or even Lucy, one day. Who knows? But right now I think I'd be too jealous of the fun my girls were having!

That said, if I were an agent then I'd be able to get Sarah some work. Lucy has definitively told me she doesn't think Sarah is a fit: sorry and all that. It's frustrating that there's nothing I can do to change her mind. Solutions keep coming into my mind, but they all seem like silly ones. I wish I didn't feel so responsible, as if it's my fault Sarah's unemployed. I try to remind myself that I'm doing more than enough for her by letting her stay with me indefinitely.

Not that it's any hardship for me, of course. I can get professional massage from Hannah any time I like, but not with the intimacy Sarah offers. And certainly not with the inevitable happy ending either! There are times when I wonder if my poor vagina will get worn out: she's certainly never been tested quite like this. But she's holding up really well.

It's great fun house-hunting with Sarah. It feels a bit like being a married couple, and I keep asking her what she thinks of places. She's happy to tell me, but keeps having to remind me that it's my apartment and my decision. "I don't think I should have a say, honey," she says over and over.

What makes it even better is that there's no hurry. I don't have to worry about aligning lease dates exactly, because if my rent overlaps by a month then my bank account will barely feel it. I can be as slow or as whimsical as I like, pretty much. After all, I can cover a month's rent on my current place in one good evening's work.

Some of the agents who show us round spacious, beautiful penthouses obviously think we're time-wasters. Two girls, doing a lot of whispering and giggling, who are far too young to fit the usual client profile. That only makes us want to wind them up even more, and we develop some great routines in which we audibly compare notes on our respective 'pub jobs'.

But then, one Thursday lunchtime, we arrive somewhere that makes us stop kidding around. It's in the middle of the area I've been mildly obsessed with: in the heart of the city, tucked away behind the shops and restaurant next to the Tower of London. I'm a sucker for a balcony and a view, and this place has both. There's a balcony that runs all the way across the living area and master (or mistress, in this case) bedroom, and there's a stunning vista of Tower Bridge. For the location and sense of place alone, the place seems like a bargain.

I like that it's fully furnished by someone who obviously knew what they were doing. Plenty of whitewash is complemented by blue leather sofas, red cushions and throws, and some gorgeously funky lamps standing free and tall on the floor's big blue tiles. There's a large glass-and-mahogany coffee table within reach, yet there's a pleasing lack of clutter. Deep down I'm a minimalist, and I like the whole open-plan vibe. It's bright and cheerful and modern, yet the few pieces of art on the walls — I'm not expert enough to say who painted them — are floral enough to keep the girly girl in me happy. I'm certain the interior designer must have been gay.

Even better, the agent guy tells us that the furniture can be bought as a job lot before moving in. It's a genius idea….why don't more places think of that? I mean, I hate the old stuff I inherited from various family members, which is currently jumbling up my Putney place. I'd be nuts to drag it over here if I can just make all this stuff — already here and really, really working — my own for good.

"Er…what do you think so far? Honestly?" I ask Sarah after a spell standing entranced at the French door. She can tell I'm serious, and I think the agent can too. A balding little guy with stupidly pointy shoes that he's shined to within an inch of their lives, he shifts his weight while pretending not to eavesdrop.

"It's a winner," comes her firm reply. She doesn't bother to keep her voice down. We're renting, not buying, after all. "It's so spacious and airy…and you'd never have to cook with all those restaurants downstairs. And hey, look up: I know you love your skylights!"

I cast my eyes to the ceiling. Can't believe I didn't notice that. We're on the top floor of the building and there's natural light from above. Sarah's really useful!

"Two spare bedrooms for visitors," she goes on. "I mean, you could even start working from home!"

"Shhh!" I hiss. I'm already not quite sure what I'm going to say when they want to check my employment and credit. I think landlords prefer full-time salaried people with job contracts. And they probably prefer to think their tenants are doing something respectable, too. I'm sure Lucy will have ideas though. She always does.

"Maybe *you* could work from home!" I grin, in a much lower whisper. "And then I'll start charging you rent."

"Haha, let's get back to the subject at hand then," she says, bringing me back to the business of flat-renting. "Listen, it won't be available for long. But it's your call, O Rich Mistress!"

She's really good at keeping my feet on the ground with her teasing, yet without ever seeming ungrateful. I need it: I don't ever want to get big-headed. I've told her more than once to shoot me if I ever turn into a Petra.

"Good point about the space though," I say. "Latifa and Alyssia are coming to town soon, and I'm thinking it would be an awful squeeze in the flat I've got right now. We could have a dance party in here!"

Sarah just winks at me and takes me by the hand, ignoring the agent's surprised look. He knows better than to follow us.

"I believe you haven't seen the main bathroom," she says, leading me through the bedroom. She's definitely being more assertive than usual about this place, which makes me feel good about it. "I snuck a peek while you were daydreaming at the window and..."

We step into a vast room and I reel. Lit up by another skylight, it's bright and big and fucking amazing. The toilet's in a separate little room, which means what we're standing in is simply a temple to bathing. It's unreal. The shower is one of those terrific things with a massive head that looks capable of producing a waterfall to rival Niagara. And there are two of them, in case you were feeling sociable. The door is clear Perspex, and the dark blue tiles — same as the living area — are flush both sides of the door.

My eye turns to the twin sinks in front of me and a vast mirror that covers the wall in front of them. But what I see to my left sells the apartment once and for all. In front of a floor-to-ceiling glass window is a vast bath. To my untrained eye, it's got all the taps and bubbling gear and lights you could ever wish for.

On three sides, anyway. It takes a while to sink in, but I realise that the fourth side is, quite simply, the window pane. The bath is so wide that you could turn sideways, switch on the Jacuzzi and look straight out onto the river, the passing boats and the Tower Bridge away to the left.

"I've never seen anything like it," I murmur. "But what if—"

"Haha, it's definitely super-strong one-way glass!" Sarah assures me. Though I'm not sure when she became an expert on modern construction materials.

"Yeah, I hope so," I respond, still gaping. "Because I could get spooked otherwise. Imagine the glass shatters and your naked self ends up eleven floors down on the street! I'm excited to try it though."

"Ooh, does that mean you're taking it?"

I grin. "I'm taking it."

She plants a quick kiss on my lips. "An excellent choice, Miss Carling. I can't wait to climb into that tub with you and a bottle of bubbly."

I smile at her again, stride out of the room and tell the agent I'll rent the apartment.

We move in just one week! Lucy (of course) has fiddled some vague but professional-looking paperwork to take care of my references, so the deal stuck easily. I give my notice on my Putney flat and, yes, I'll have to pay rent twice in November.

But that's hardly much of a worry. I'm really quite overwhelmed by my income still, and the scary thing is that I kept my apartment shopping pretty reasonable compared to what I might have done. I'm going to have loads left over every month, and I really don't know what to do with it yet.

My thoughts run to a few other people (besides Sarah) who could use help, or at least a coffee or two. Even my parents, who keep complaining — I never know if I should take it seriously — about how tight things are in retirement. Penthouses and good food and taking care of myself aside, I don't think I need much. I'm not particularly tempted to buy a car just for the sake of it, really I'm not. The idea of becoming prostitution's answer to Robin Hood is actually more appealing. I like it a lot.

But there's a big problem, and that's that if I start throwing my money around, people will ask questions about where it came from. Though my conscience is clear, I still care too much about what people will say and think if they know the truth.

Apart from that, I can hardly think of anything to worry about as I survey my little dump of a flat and imagine how much time it's going to take me (okay, a bit of me and a lot of Sarah) to pack it all up in some kind of order. Life is pretty awesome if that's all I've got to worry about.

Then a shrill text tone — followed by another — shatters my peace. It's Lucy. My pain results are in. I scored terrifically well, apparently. I can take anything her toughest girls can take. It makes me nervous but proud.

I scroll to the next text. It's a second one from my lovely agent. But what I read makes my blood go cold. I'm to be blindfolded and taken to the mysterious suburban house again. The one where I heard those terrifying words.

I know you, Emma Carling. I've known you a very long time.

And this time, I'll be going alone.

XI

I'm back in that room. The one that feels enormous, reeks of wealth and sounds utterly ominous. That last one is the silence talking. And my blindfold, which makes the quiet seem louder. The thick cloth is tighter than before, but my brain still strains for the sight it knows it will be denied.

The only sounds are those of footsteps and breathing. Both are heavier than the last time I was in this place, and I sense a heightened urgency. Previously it was five of us here, subjected to an intimate inspection; now it's just me. I'm not sure if that makes me some kind of chosen one. Lucky or unlucky? I've got very few answers right now.

That Esmeralda woman is in the room once again. I think that she's the only other person present, apart from him. She's been giving me my instructions since I arrived, whilst he's presumably been the one doing the things I can't do for myself.

Things such as putting the cuffs onto my wrists and tightening them hard. Things like raising my arms above my head and attaching the chain to some kind of wall fastening in front of me.

My body began to quiver when he did that, almost the moment I felt the stretch tug through me. For all my training, I've never been put into exactly this position.

The cuffs are so unrelenting on my wrists that I can pull all my weight through them and nothing budges. But then it hurts more, the metal cutting into my skin like a savage old tin opener.

I can make my wrists comfortable if I stand on the tips of my toes. But that, too, is not a position I can hold for long. I have to keep altering my pose, and my heart thuds at this, my first real bondage test as a professional. The discomfort and the anticipation at least make me forget my reservations about this particular client for a moment.

As per my rather unusual brief, I'm wearing something suitable for working in an office. It's one of my most faithful (and unimaginative) blouse-and-skirt combinations, in fact. It's a thrilling reminder of just how far I've come. I could easily be wearing this in some dull company tomorrow, but apparently this workaday outfit, so far from sexy, is actually able to get somebody going. So too, I suppose, are the almost industrial bra and panties I was specifically delivered for this job. The plot thickens in my mind.

I can smell a lot of leather, but it's not furniture. My guess is that I'm up close to — but not touching — a bookshelf. Probably the kind of men's club thing that's stuffed with dusty, expensive volumes nobody reads. Law books, maybe, or something equally uninspiring. But that smell of old-school binding, along with the scent of wood, fires up the image of comfortable decadence in my mind. Cranleigh House decadence.

There's a rustle behind me and *he* is suddenly against my body. I gasp and sway on my shackle, semi-suspended as he knocks me off-balance. There's a violent urgency about the contact he makes with me. I sense he is a great deal taller than I am, as he presses against me with a hard swelling that nudges furiously against my skirt from behind. An elbow crooks around my ribs as his left hand takes hold of my throat and squeezes, just hard enough for me to tense.

Another hand slips around the front of my skirt, and I feel something rising in me now. I'm into the moment already, and my concerns fade into distant memory as the hand plays across the fuzzy material, rubbing down into my cleft once or twice. Then it grabs a fistful of skirt and pulls hard, exposing the front of my thighs. Once he has yanked the garment up, he slithers his wrist beneath it.

My knees weaken even further as long, artful fingers descend on that thick underwear of mine, caressing firmly along what I know is already a damp valley. The friction of the unsubtle textile is hot and rough. I like it more than I expect to, and I moan.

As the sound escapes my mouth, there's a tiny snort behind me. There's no denying it's derisive: it's right behind my ear. Close enough to smell its venom. There's amusement in its tone, but there's nothing friendly about it. I should be worried, I know, but then the grip on my throat tightens further and two fingers dive beneath the sodden fabric down there. The palm crosses my professionally manicured patch and the digits curl inside my wetness, a sudden and welcome invasion of my body.

I try not to groan this time, but can't help sucking in a juicy lungful of air as my lower lip drops open with the weight of the passion I'm feeling. Behind my blindfold, instinct takes over and my eyes close.

Then the hands are gone from my throat and my pussy. The hips move away from mine, and there's no more hardness pressing against me from behind. I hold that breath, desperate to know what's coming next. Even while loving the not knowing.

A few seconds pass, and once again I become aware of the distant spark and crackle of a fireplace in use. I feel warmer than I did last time, but then I'm fully dressed. But not for long. There's a step forward and this time the skirt is lifted from behind. Two hands —

the same two hands, so huge and powerful in my mind — enter purposefully, diving over the elastic above my buttocks like dolphins leaping in surf. They take hold and they pull.

The fabric doesn't stand a chance, despite its thickness. I can hear and feel the rip. When he pulls the limp, moist rag between my legs and out beneath my skirt, it burns my lips a little. I'm waiting for him to rip open the skirt too — which will piss me off, because it's mine — but instead he reaches around and unclips it. The respect comes as a slight surprise.

The skirt drops to the floor, and now I'm naked from the waist down apart from the flat, grey shoes I'm sporting. Another item from my collection of comfortable office favourites that I've thought better than to throw in the bin.

Next comes one of Esmeralda's mechanical instructions, delivered in her sexy and hard-to-place accent. Dutifully I slide my legs apart, until she tells me to stop. It feels like there's a yard of space between them, but it may not be that much in reality. Whatever the truth, it's becoming difficult to keep standing straight.

There's a tinkle and a clink of metal behind me. A hand grips my right ankle, and then I feel the steel. A tight ring clamps around the bone, quickly followed by the same on the left. As the hands run gently up the outsides of my calves, I cautiously try to feel out what has been done to me.

I can't really move my ankles, but it doesn't feel like they're shackled to the wall the way my wrists are. There's resistance between them, and so I suspect it's a kind of metal bar designed to keep my feet spaced exactly as they are. I know these things have a name, but all I can do is picture it. Another little device we didn't get to try in school.

But then, after I'm told to bend at the waist, so that everything within me is pulling, straining and paining my body, comes something I'm well prepared for.

My submissive juices are flowing like sweet honey as I hang

there, hurting just enough to feel a thrill. Esmeralda seems to come over to me, although I am pretty sure *he* is still very close. She's right behind me now, and tells me I need to keep absolutely still.

I hear a slurpy liquid noise, like the gentle squeeze of toothpaste from a tube. Only it's not toothpaste, of course. It's lubricant. And Esmeralda is the one administering it. The deft little fingers are definitely not the same. Guess the big man doesn't want to get his hands dirty.

I wonder if it's a turn-on for a man to have a female prepare another woman's anus for his entry? Silly question, I guess. As one, and then two of her fingers gently squirm and stretch inside me, I realise that I've missed this. Apart from the unpleasant call at Doctor Krasznik's rooms, it's been a while since I've had it in there.

Stupidly, I blush at the thought: maybe this little English girl isn't quite shameless enough yet to contemplate her own sighing satisfaction at a couple of fingers in her ass without turning crimson.

Whatever, I find myself pushing back in towards her and loving every second of this feeling. It's like it's ten times better for being tied up, rooted in place with my legs spread and a man — whose incredible proportions are reaching masterpiece levels in my mind's eye — watches me being opened up for him.

In this position I can let my neck hang absolutely limp, and there's something intoxicating about it. It makes me feel like the wanton rag doll I so enjoy being. My breathing quickens when she withdraws at last. Instinctively I try to widen my legs, inviting re-entry, but that bar won't let me do it.

This time two chuckles come. She's laughing with him! Why do they find my need amusing? I hear more tinkling metal, and I pray it's a belt loosening. I'm waiting for a zip, and the treat that should emerge from it, with such fervour that I can smell my own wetness rising up from between my legs.

With other clients, I'm guessing I'd be begging by now, just as Miss Jackson would want me to. But it doesn't seem appropriate here. Especially if they're going to take a sadistic kind of pleasure in my volcanic desire. I try to wait quietly and patiently instead.

I hear Esmeralda walk away.

I'm still trying to stop myself from panting audibly when the first blow crashes into my back.

Shit! I've been tricked. This isn't anal entry at all. This is a belting. The weapon barely notices the blouse I'm wearing, and my skin sears and stings in the pause that follows the first hit.

There's a different kind of panting behind me now. One that suggests the mildest of physical effort.

Crack! I jolt violently as another one lands, lengthways between my shoulder blades once more. My crazed, off-the-charts session with Rupert and Petra comes flooding back to my mind. So do my moments with Carrie, when I was thrashed with my head in Miss Jackson's fireplace.

Before the third blow, his hand leaps below my blouse and rips off my bra in a single move. He grabs a nipples and he twists. I can feel the hardness in the way it resists his heavy pressure, and I gasp.

I want it all. That twist, the belt, the cock to get inside in my ass. I clench my teeth as I become more beautifully aware of the tightness of my bonds, the wetness in both my holes and the screaming of my breasts. The belt lashes me again. I cry a little whimper, but I know I can take this. It's only a belt. The after-sting, which spreads slowly, is worse than the actual strike.

I can't deny that the withdrawal of sight is immersing me in my wonderful work like nothing else. Two more exquisite hits rain down upon me, and I actually feel my mouth curl into a smile. The release is going to be incredible, when it comes. Oh, I'm one depraved little girl, that's for sure.

And then time stands still. There's no release, and I freeze. Because he stops the whipping and leans right over me, his sweat-soaked shirt meshing with mine, and pushes hard enough that I give a cry as my hips collapse. All my weight pulses through my wrists as

I struggle to regain a posture. My suffering hands are screaming for circulation above my head.

That whisper again. Louder than last time, but just as hot and just as scary.

"I see you've found yourself a nice new job, Emma Carling. I always knew you were a dirty little whore deep inside. Oh yes, I could see it in your eyes when you were thirteen."

Suddenly I feel horrified. I want to tear off my mask and know who this man is that claims to know my life and my work. Fuck! I must know!

"Who are you?" I find myself asking, summoning up my voice for the first time all night. I'm trying to sound more professional than I feel, reminding myself that tonight, at £3000, is my biggest payday since my debut with Charles.

This time there's neither a snort nor a snicker. Just an other-worldly growl of a laugh. From deep in the throat, like the sound of a snoring bear, it really could be anybody. It resonates with nastiness and superiority, but there's no other clue I can glean.

It's Esmeralda who finally answers: "You will know when the time is right, Emma Carling."

I say nothing. But I swear you could hear the beat of my heart and the gush of my adrenaline from across the street.

Without another word, he stands up, pulls apart my cheeks and inserts himself quickly — too quickly — into my ass. My desire now consumed by fear, I have to work hard to keep steady as he pounds me with an enormous length that tests my limits. My chains clank all the while as he repeatedly rams into me, my body thrown forward each time while my ankles are rooted into their places.

I grit my teeth. I know the monster enjoys the idea that I don't enjoy it; that he's spoiled what I was looking forward to with his sudden entry and hurtful pounding. He comes inside me with a loud, primal grunt. He has possessed me and taken every piece of me that he can. On *his* terms. I feel the heat of his satisfaction coursing through my back hole.

And me? I don't know what I'm feeling. It's also something primal, but is it fight or is it flight? Fear or fascination? I'm a tangle.

As he slowly twitches back to normality within me, and tears try to attack my eyes, he leans in once more and delivers a frightening double entendre in that same trademark whisper.

"Consider yourself fucked, Emma Carling."

XII

I'm tempted to wake Sarah when I get home, sweaty, sore and upset. But she's fast asleep and looking angelic enough to calm me down. I feel tearful again as I look at her face, because she's part of this new dream life. A life I suddenly fear may have to end.

I lie awake all night thinking about it. I was doing so well, and everything was perfect. But now these mind games are back. This guy is playing with me and I don't know what to do. Are the things he says par for the course in this game? I can't believe it's okay: it just doesn't add up with anything Lucy has told me about client discretion and all of that.

Then again, this is a situation she hasn't really prepared me for in any of our chats. Maybe it's a first for her, too. She's been vague about this client in a way that's completely different to the others. She's been nervous about this job since day one, and usually thoughtful and detailed briefs have been patchy. I wasn't specifically warned about potential violence tonight, not that I minded.

On the contrary, the whole physical side was amazing. Despite my worried state, a small part of what's keeping me up is replays of what happened before things got weird at the end. I'm totally good with the blindfolds and the shackles and the belts and the spacer bar thing on my ankles. It rocked.

The mystery of it all would be brilliant if he didn't go and whisper the things he does. Maybe it's a turn-on to say things like that to a hooker? Maybe everyone does it? Hmm, but the guy knows my full name and knows that I'm recently unemployed. And Lucy specifically told me she wouldn't give out those kinds of personal details.

The obvious thing is to talk to her. Of all people, I should be completely comfortable chatting to her. If he's a new client, and he's going over a line, then she needs to know. Even Lucy could make a mistake by taking on a bad egg, I suppose. She won't know if I don't tell her! And what if he's crossed the ultimate line and taken photos? My mind is in overdrive.

But something wants to hold me back from talking to Lucy. Aren't I being silly? The only thing to spoil my night was words. And aren't words at the very bottom of the list of things for a prostitute to worry about? Maybe all the girls get this kind of talk, and I'm over-reacting. And anyway, if the guy wants to ruin me then he's already got enough to work with. I may as well keep taking his money if it's on offer.

I fear I'm over-rationalising about something that's really quite clear-cut. Perhaps the main thing making me hesitate is that I don't want to let Lucy down. I'm still one of the new girls, and I don't feel confident enough to go to her and complain about one of the jobs she's kindly arranged for me. Especially such a lucrative one. Shouldn't I be strong and suck it up?

The question of who it might be haunts me well into the next day, as I sit grumpily with Sarah and wonder if I should cancel the new flat and get out of this crazy new world I'm in. I'm clearly out of my depth, I warble. For once, she's silent. But only for a moment. Then she says: "You're cooked in the head if you don't talk to Lucy about this," and underlines her point by walking away into the kitchen.

Who could it be? That's what I want to know. An assortment of ex-boyfriends, teachers, family friends and school friends cruise through my head on a conveyer belt. Colleagues seem to be ruled out, since this person claims they've known me since my teens. I can't think of anybody I've worked with who falls into that category.

It could easily be one of the sweetest, kindest people I know, couldn't it? It could be a quiet soul that I'd never suspect. The unlikely ones are the ones who turn out to be kinkiest. Maybe someone religious? An enemy? I'm stumped. And he has to be rich, judging by the length of the gravel driveway I've been taken down at his property, not to mention the length of time it takes to walk across the room where all the action seems to happen.

The thought that really drives me insane is that it could be someone who knows my parents. But would he really want to embarrass me? What would be the point? Blackmail? No – he's loaded. Power trip? Now *that's* possible. Maybe it's just the pleasure of playing mind games.

"I'm not smart enough for all this spy movie stuff," I moan to Sarah as she walks back in with another cup of tea for me. "I don't know the first thing about bluffs and double-bluffs. Fuck, what do I do?"

"You're asking the wrong girl, Missy. You need an expert. If you really won't speak to Lucy, how about Miss Jackson? Haven't you been trying to get around to meeting her?"

True, I could sound her out, hopefully without giving too much away. There's a new paranoia growing in me that saying something to someone will be exactly what might set my 'outing' in motion. I'm scared. Maybe Miss Jackson might let something slip after a drink or two. Not that I have any idea what alcohol might do to her.

I nod thoughtfully as Sarah puts my tea down on the table and gives me a hug. Again, she asks me to talk through every detail of the night.

When I finish, she clears her throat: "You really found it hot, though, didn't you?"

"Mostly – until the end bit," I admit.

"It's the first kinky customer you've had, isn't it?"

"Yeah."

Her eyes light up.

"You know, I can think of another reason you don't want to go to Lucy. You enjoy it too much. You like the bad boy, much as he might upset you at times. And you know that Lucy will strike him off the client list the moment you put in a complaint."

I look at her: "You're crazy!"

She cocks her head. "And you're dirty. I know you pretty well now, Emma Carling. I think you like having the naughty and the nice!"

"What's the nice part?"

"Charles. He's your angel, and this other guy is your demon. You've got both pieces of the pie in your hands, and you don't want to lose one of them. Speaking of which, you've got Charles again tonight, haven't you?"

"You're right. About my appointment, I mean. I'm not sure about the rest of your theory."

"Mark my words," she tuts, going into drama mode again. "Emma Carling doesn't know the depths of her own depravity — haha, excuse the pun if you will!"

I think she's being silly, but she does make me feel better. And yes, Charles will be pure pleasure and take my mind off things. In fact, it's not beyond the realms of possibility that I could pick his brains a little. He's supposed to have friends in this world, after all.

And I set up a chat with Miss Jackson for the next day. There's something resembling a plan in place, and that's a relief. For now, I'll keep Lucy out of this whole thing. Just for now.

∽

Charles has decided he wants me once a week. He's booked me in for every Friday evening that I'm available, for the exorbitant fee of £4000. It's not far off what he paid for my opening night in the game.

"If he wants to book you for a regular slot," explains Lucy, "then he's got to pay over the odds for it. We have to cover what we'd make from people his booking makes us turn away. Especially as Fridays are popular nights.

"And besides," I can hear her grinning down the phone line, "That's what he thinks you're worth anyway, you starlet!"

I don't tell her that I'm getting to the point that I'd happily spend my Friday nights with Charles for nothing. Getting paid to do what you love — or do whom you love — well, that's the dream, isn't it? So I keep my mouth shut and remind myself of what a lucky girl I am. Just one of those nights with him, after all, will cover the month's rent on my new place. Not to mention a few hundred Pounds of beer money.

Thinking of the numbers makes me feel ever less inclined to rock the proverbial boat. This isn't minimum wage work: I should take the good with the bad, shouldn't I? And maybe Sarah's right: There's definitely a good side to the bad side. I think.

Charles finally spanks me on our fourth night together, the second of our regular Friday appointments. He has no wish to really damage me, he says, but he enjoys putting a girl over his knee sometimes. I am more than good with that. But although I like it a lot, it's really the expert fingering he gives me afterwards that makes me come.

That's the thing with Charles. We connect emotionally and share a lot, to the point that my feelings for him make my heart and soul melt. So much so that I feel terrible about taking his cash. He is a master in bed, and puts more effort into satisfying me than into looking after himself. In my limited experience, that's not common practice.

But Charles is a shit dominant.

I hate to have to say it, because I want him to be perfect at that, too, like he is at everything else. If I were looking for someone to marry, or a man to sleep with five nights a week, he'd be my winner right now. He's incredibly well-groomed and tasteful, and he has the most delicious cock of them all. It's clean, shaven and free of ugly veins. I love to lick it the way I would an ice cream, running my tongue across the succulent balls and nibbling on tiny mouthfuls of skin. I love to lick his ass, too, and find myself stuffing as much of my tongue in there as I can.

I can keep going for hours on Charles, loving every moment. And the great thing is, so can he.

But he can't dish out convincing punishment. He's too nice. It's fun, but there isn't the same edge I get with, say…*him.*

I'm trying not to think of my latest night in a blindfold, but I'm finding it hard in more ways than one. Even that anal attack, which came while I was twitching with worry, has now joined the pantheon of my erotic fantasy bank. Part of me wishes the memory wasn't so arousing, but then — as Sarah so kindly observed — it doesn't seem like I get a say in my mind's depraved wanderings.

The things I'm learning about myself each day…I suspect that none of them would please the feminists of this world.

But if I'm looking for an all-round night of glorious, uninhibited, straight sex, then the dextrous, multi-skilled Charles is my man of choice right now. He keeps on insisting on cooking me dinner. It's part of the 'girlfriend experience' he craves and could so easily have for free.

"It's never free, though, is it?" he says mysteriously when I question him. "Once you get into a relationship, you pay a price in other ways."

I nod thoughtfully, increasingly receptive to his point of view. But I swear that I'm going to cook for him soon. Just the moment I get round to doing that kitchen course I promised I'd do. I've vowed to be useful and improve myself during my ample free time, and I intend to.

"How about you learn to make sushi?" suggests Charles as he stirs a bubbling ratatouille. "I'll eat it off your naked body. Deal?"

I smile. I've heard of that odd practice. Could be fun, especially if the food is prepared by my loving hands. "Deal," I smile, with a little shiver of anticipation.

We talk about so much more than sex, and usually we don't get down to business before midnight and a few sherries on the sofa have come and gone. He really enjoys the slow build. I love it too.

He tells me secrets about his work — only three days a week at his one man stock market consultancy — and I share a lot about my own life. I trust him implicitly. Even if it turned out that Charles knew my dad, I wouldn't worry that he'd blab. There's an amazing respect there.

I can't speak much about my current work, of course, because discretion is understood and implicit in all of my encounters. Still, as long as I don't mention names or places, I can tell the odd tale that makes my face go red.

I don't want to say anything about the mystery gentleman and blindfold house, though. Charles and Lucy are too close. But I ask a few general questions, trying to engineer that conversation so that the topics I want come up naturally.

Does he know of men who like to psychologically torture their escorts? Or men who keep their faces a secret? Is that a thing?

"I certainly do know of gentlemen who will hide their faces," says Charles. "One friend of mine is so careful that he won't reveal himself to the girl he's had every week for the past five years! Venetian masks tend to be quite popular for hiding oneself. There's a sexy and alluring mystery about those that everyone seems to love.

"Other men prefer to blindfold the girl, but a lot of them worry that she might sneak a peek at them. This friend is one of them. A very well-known public figure. You wouldn't believe if I told you."

"I bet the girls can usually find out one way or another, can't they? I mean, there's always some gossip out there, isn't there?"

"It happens, sure. But not as much as you might think. Sometimes even agents don't know whom they're dealing with. They get contacted by a PA or a lackey who transfers the money and sends the instructions. I don't think that's safe though – Lucy's insistence on knowing whom you're going to sleep with is ideal for your safety. She's done very well to earn so much trust.

"The code of understanding is very effective in this business, remember. Considering that nearly everyone in the upper strata of society has something that they'd like to hide — the kind of thing newspapers like to write about — everyone knows it's not wise to spread rumours. It will almost certainly backfire. It's a bit like the Cold War, really. Don't fire, because it'll come right back at you.

"Never be tempted," he goes on. "No matter how perfect and skilled you are at what you do, rumours that you're indiscreet in *any* way will amount to professional suicide."

I pause. "I get that. But at the same time…I could tell Lucy if somebody made me uncomfortable, couldn't I?"

He sits up in mock horror, whipping his hand off my thigh like greased lightning. "Why, what have I done?"

"Don't be silly, Charles, you're perfect, I can assure you!"

And he really is. I mean, he's even told me that he's put all the other girls he used to see out to pasture. One night a week with me is all he needs. It's the whoring equivalent of a marriage proposal, I suppose, and it does something similar to me.

He relaxes again and, this time, puts his arm around my shoulder. "Of course, you'd tell Lucy anything. Your agent is part of your business and needs to know everything. Like I said, she's discretion personified." His eyes narrow suspiciously. "Why do you ask? Has someone been making my Emma unhappy?"

Fuck. I didn't engineer that very well. Damn amontillado. "No, no," I say in a hurry. "I mean, everything is new, and I'm still just figuring out what's normal…"

He doesn't look convinced, but I can tell he won't pester me. He knows I wouldn't like that. So I'm emboldened to push on with the questions.

"What about the psychological games thing?"

"That happens, too, and could take a lot of forms," he replies. "I have heard of a couple of men who occasionally take a girl for verbal abuse and don't even touch them." He stops for a moment and shakes his head. "What a waste! There are some very weird ones out there."

"I'm not surprised by that! Can't wait for that booking to come in...not!"

He chuckles, and I think he's now sold on the idea that I'm just asking hypothetical questions.

"There's another thing I worry about," I say, feeling the tips of my ears go warm. "What if a client recognised me? Or knew me?"

"You mean you turn up to a booking and it turns out that the guy is your family dentist?" he grins.

His words bring the unwelcome image of Doctor Fisher to my mind's eye. Dentists: they earn pretty well, don't they? And he *has* known me most of my life...

"Hello? Emma?"

Jeez, I've just slipped into a reverie about whether he could in fact be Doctor Fisher, the man who prodded relentlessly in my mouth from an early age, and who made me wear braces for a year in my teens. He could hardly have chosen a more disturbing example.

"Erm, sorry! Yes! That's *exactly* what I mean."

"Look, it can happen, for sure. Sometimes London isn't as big as you want it to be. In fact, I once had a girl who was in my class at school!"

My eyes turn to saucers. "Wow! And...?"

"We had a laugh about it the moment she walked in, pretty much. I had no clue she had gone into that line of work. We had a good time comparing notes about how well we were getting on in life, in our own very different ways. Then she admitted she'd actually fancied me in school! So it ended pretty well..."

I actually feel a bizarre twinge of jealously as he speaks about sleeping with another woman. I try and slap it out. Rupert feelings are a bad idea. I know that. I can love, but not jealously. I can love, but never take anything for granted.

"Well, it's good to know that it doesn't have to be horribly embarrassing every time, at least."

"Absolutely," he says in a cheery tone. "The more you're honest — within the boundaries of discretion — the better off you'll be, Emma. Be proud of what you do."

"Yeah, that's easy to say! Have you told your mum that you use prostitutes and are never going to get married?"

It's a rather personal question, but I feel comfortable enough with him to ask it.

"Actually I have, as a matter of fact," he admits. "She's not thrilled about it, but trust me, it's so much better not to keep secrets about yourself. We even have the odd jibe about it now. Hey, maybe I'll take you over to meet her next Friday!"

"Don't you dare," I snap, safe in the knowledge that he's kidding.

He laughs, and I decided there and then that we've chatted enough. Proudly and spontaneously doing the initiative thing Miss Jackson loves so much, I sink to my knees in front of where he sits on the sofa. I begin to massage the bulge in his trousers, then set about undoing that Louis Vuitton belt of his.

XIII

alking through Hyde Park with Miss Jackson makes me feel like one of those quintessentially English 'ladies who lunch'. As a hard-working, no-frills London girl, the thought is almost — but not quite — as embarrassing as the idea that I'm a full-blown prostitute.

But there's no escaping the fact that I've never had so much free time on my hands. And, like the prostitute thing, I'm kidding myself if I pretend it isn't kinda nice. I never knew you could have so many coffee and lunch dates in the middle of a weekday, but I love that I can.

It's a crisp, mild Monday afternoon, and the sky is blue as we enjoy the early winter sun on our backs. Cyclists and joggers weave past us in their own haughty way, while we saunter past children feeding ducks. None of our fellow park-goers could possibly guess — not in their wildest imagination — the bizarre relationship between these two innocent-looking (I hope) women out on a stroll. It's surreal for me to think about it. Especially with the image of my companion's moist, pink pussy in my face so fresh in my mind.

This should be weird and awkward, after all these weeks. A

teacher and a former student, meeting together for social chit-chat. But Miss Jackson — who is now trying to teach me to call her Miranda — makes it all seem perfectly normal. She cracks a few jokes and confronts the elephants that would otherwise be clogging up the proverbial room. She even compliments me on how well I did that day. The day she sat back on top of her desk and spread her legs before me, of course.

Soon, nothing seems remotely awkward any more. And I shouldn't be surprised by that. Miranda Jackson — I can't get used to the first-name thing at all — is the one woman whose wisdom and way with words can put even Lucy's into the shade. I have been in awe of her since day one at training, but now the slight barrier of her assessing my every move is gone. She's treating me as an equal, yet sharing her knowledge without ever coming across as superior.

She wants to hear all of my stories. That's another thing that shouldn't surprise me, given this is the woman who so clearly enjoyed watching my sexual antics on screen and in person. I share a few juicy tales with her, and she mockingly chides me for looking over my shoulder before I embark on the really lewd parts.

"Sorry," I mutter, coming over terribly English again. "I'm getting there, really I am. I'm starting to think about telling my parents, at last. Seriously."

She stops and looks me in the eye for a moment. "I hope so," she says. "And good for you. You should be proud. Remember, I'd love to do what you do. I just don't quite have the look for it."

She smiles, and gazes up at a red-and-yellow kite flapping above the treetops. I look at the noble Miss Jackson. I've never thought she might have desires like that, somehow. I don't know what I thought, but definitely not that. It's probably true, what she says. Her look is not only on the plain side, but it's far from girly. In fact, following our encounter in the office, I assumed I was right in assessing her as a lesbian.

"Are you…bisexual, then?" I ask, a little timidly. Although I know perfectly well she's not going to get offended.

"I'm more lesbian, to be honest," she says. "That's the other problem I'd have. Women don't pay for sex all that much." She sighs. "And that's a shame. But you can't go changing the laws of supply and demand when it comes to nature! And if I did men, then I'd have to do a lot of faking. And as you were very well taught, that's a long way from professional."

"I guess so," I agree. I'm finding it odd to feel sympathy for Miss Jackson. "How did you become a mentor at Cranleigh then?"

"I used to do what Lucy does. My method was a little unusual, though, because I would always go along and watch my girls in action. It gave me peace of mind that they were safe, and — funnily enough — the men loved it. It added to their fantasy that their girl was a slave and I was her keeper. So that was my speciality."

"Wow!" is all I can muster. There's so much I want to ask. But she goes on without me needing to.

"Anyway, doing things that way gave me incredible insight into what the males want and how they respond. Or even couples, on occasion. I learned what girls do right and wrong. A rare privilege, because for all the great work they do, not many agents actually see their girls in action.

"When Cranleigh started its operation seven years ago, I was about ready to stop working full-time. Doing a couple of courses a year at the school, where I could share my knowledge constructively, was the perfect way for me to start winding down. Only I've ended up staying a little longer than planned. I just love meeting the new talent too much!"

Cranleigh House...I'm still mad with curiosity about that place. Such a shame it's the epitome of discretion and all that.

"I'm not going to get much more out of you where details of who's who in that school are concerned, am I?" I ask her with a wry grin.

She laughs. "You know I can't, Emma. All I will say is, keep your ears and eyes open. Everyone knows everyone in our world, and sooner or later someone may let something slip. Or you'll just make a connection for yourself. It'll be a eureka moment for you. Something to look forward to."

"So I might figure out who owns the place at some point?"

She purses her lips. "Maybe…"

"Do you really think I might run into anybody who worked or mentored…or whatever you'd call it…in my new job?"

"It's a possibility, yes," she says, with admirable patience. "But you've met them anyway, Emma!"

"I know I have. I just…I'd love to know if there's a hierarchy. Or if there are people involved that I never even saw. And what some of the men are like when they're not in teacher mode. I mean, how many people were playing roles? And what about that guy who woke us up each day?"

"Your fascination with individual men lives on, I see, Miss Carling," she says, suddenly going all sage and teacher-like on me. I feel like I'm back in her office, in trouble again. But then she grins. "Not still thinking of Rupert, are we? Oh dear, I really hope you're not falling for clients like you did for him…"

I go red as I think of Charles, and wonder if it is quite the same. Would I cry, now, if he cancelled on me or took my clothes or suddenly treated me like the whore I really am? I've got a feeling that I'd be stronger this time around. But her words are a timely reminder to watch myself.

I change tack slightly, coming to the one thing I'm really curious about. "What about the guest speaker we had? Can you at least say anything about *him*?"

She looks at me in surprise, her head turning sharply in my direction. "Oh…it's funny you should mention that."

My blood runs cold.

"He asked about you."

I stop walking straight away.

"What?!" I yelp.

I'm completely forgetting that I'm supposed to be staying cool about this.

"Yes, I remember now," she muses. "As I was showing him out, he asked if that brunette's name was Emma Carling."

Fuck! And fuck again. The expletives are stampeding in my head. So that bastard, Spurring, most definitely did recognise me at the school. My prayer that he didn't know who the hell I was; that this particular ex-employee was utterly faceless to him, just another body on the shop floor, wasn't answered.

"Oh," I say, in what I hope is a more even tone. Though really I want to strangle her for forgetting to tell me of this vital little conversation at any point since it took place. Of all the moments for her to switch off…really! "And did you tell him?"

She frowns. "Of course not! I explained that we could never divulge personal details of any of our school learners. For similar reasons I can't tell you his name either, of course."

"I see," I murmur, my mind working furiously. Well, her confirmation would have been neither here nor there. The man recognised me — that was the point. I decide I have to come clean with Miss Jackson.

"Don't worry, I know his name already. That guy was the CEO of the company I just left before coming to the school. Still is, I presume. And I'm not sure if you might have heard, but my departure from that job wasn't exactly amicable. Or quiet."

She seems genuinely stumped for once. There's a long pause as we walk on. Finally she pulls me over to a sunny bench next to the path, and we sit down.

"I had heard that you left with a bang, Emma. But this is an incredible co-incidence. We had *no* idea you had any connection with him. I'm so sorry that happened. It's unheard of. One in a million — almost literally.

"I know I've told you to be proud, and all of that, but I can see that must be an awkward situation buzzing about in your head. I mean, of all people!"

I nod glumly, although I'm a little perked up by her understanding. I feel better to have it off my chest, though I don't think I am going to tell her any more. My suspicion that Spurring is my psychological torturer is back with a vengeance. Even if he can't possibly have known me since I was thirteen…I think?

"We'll have to be more careful with guest speakers in the future," declares Miss Jackson. "But right now I can only apologise."

I give her a weak smile. I'm not angry at her or the school. Just at my rotten luck. "It wasn't your fault. Was it his first time there?"

"Yes, we only have guest speakers as one-offs. It's a much sought-after treat for certain men in London, and it's given as a sort of client loyalty prize by an association of top agents who help us line up students—"

She clasps a hand over her mouth. "Shit, I'm saying too much here. Keep this to yourself, please, Emma."

I nod as I brush a stray autumn leaf from my lap. "Of course, of course."

It's all I needed to hear, anyway. The man regularly uses the services of whores and is clearly one of London's best-paying clients. And he's the only person I can think of who may have an issue with me after my public assault on his company and his management. Things are adding up. Holy crap. He *must* be *him*.

I wish I could seek more clues from Miss Jackson, but I know this is all I'm going to get.

Yet she does volunteer one more thing. "Emma, I don't want you to worry, okay?" She's looking me right in the eye, and apparently she's right back into mind-reading mode. "This is an unusual situation, but the laws that keep discretion in place apply now more than ever."

"Go on?" I urge her.

"You may feel concerned that he has some kind of dark secret on you, and that he might want to do you some kind of harm. But you know some secrets about him too, don't you? And he *knows* that you know them. Remember that. Who has more to lose, huh?"

She's right, I suppose. He can't doubt that I would have recognised him at Cranleigh. And if he's the one blindfolding me and threatening me, well, he's taking a massive risk on his part. Because, if memory serves, his 'corporate image' is a squeaky-clean one. For him to take the chance he's taking…this must be one almighty power trip.

All things considered, would he *really* do anything? *Could* he?

"Come," says Miranda, standing up from the bench. "Let me buy you a coffee. I'm dying to hear more wicked tales of your adventures. We can even sit outside up on Bayswater – it's such a lovely day!"

We spend the rest of the afternoon sipping lattes. And I don't have to worry about the caffeine keeping me awake all night, since that's when I do most of my work. Another very neat thing about my job.

We marvel at the weather as she listens, enraptured, to the news that Sarah is living with me, and that Latifa and Alyssia are coming to London for a visit. I ask her advice about Sarah's quest for work, and she says she thinks Lucy's being harsh. "I've watched that double penetration assignment you did with her more than once," she says, casual as if she were discussing a soap opera, "and I think she's got a lot of potential. I understand Lucy's reservations, but Sarah just needs a bit more time and practice pleasing men. I gather she's already a dream lesbian lover…"

She gives me a wink.

"Ah yes," I murmur with a smile, closing my eyes and leaning back in my metal chair. I'm surprised with the ease and candour of my reaction. "We have fun!"

"I love it!" cries Miranda Jackson. "We've obviously seen many supposedly 'straight' girls explore their bisexuality at the school with some success, but I don't think we've had something resembling a couple come out of it before. You scored in more ways than one! I really think Lucy should let the two of you work as a pair. I'd get off watching that every time. Clients would too. They're not stupid: they'd detect the chemistry between you for sure."

I shrug. "Well, Lucy's made her final decision. I already tried pleading."

"For now," admits Miss Jackson. "But Sarah can take her own initiative. And then things may change. Here, look."

She pulls out her cell phone and I lean forward to take a look. She shows me an app. It's simple enough, she explains. Men use it to find and book local prostitutes. There are photos, ratings, reviews… wow! It's pretty neat. I can't believe it hadn't occurred to us that something like that existed.

"Anybody can sign up to advertise on here," hints Miss Jackson. "And maybe one of those spare rooms in your flat could handle the odd visitor?"

I nod thoughtfully.

"Look, she won't do as well as with an agent," she says. "Because the super-rich use agents and that's that. But she could still get £300 for a session. It's good money, decent experience and great for the CV with all those public reviews. Tell her to sign up: I'd be happy to be her first client."

Once again my weird world comes sharply into focus as I look at the plain, yet strong and liberated woman in front of me, talking about paying my friend — okay, girlfriend — to have sex with her in my new flat. I'm not quite sure if she's being serious, but the most stunning thing is that I'm okay with it.

I smile. "Thank you Miss – I mean, Miranda…I'll let you know as soon as her profile is up. It's such a good idea. We should have thought about it before, really!"

Despite the unnerving revelation about Spurring, I feel light and happy. Things are looking up. Miranda Jackson has put a positive spin on everything, and I can't wait to tell Sarah her great new idea when I get home.

XIV

The scene is one of utter chaos. People are whooping, hollering and just about knocking each other over. Beyond all the squealing and screeching, my hallway is littered with boxes and bags. It's a noisy mess.

I've just moved into my new flat. And if that isn't confusing enough, Latifa and Alyssia have just arrived. The volcanic energy of their greeting is a reminder of what a hectic few days this is going to be. Maybe I should have thought twice about moving house on the same day as their arrival. I haven't even unpacked yet!

The hugs and kisses — on the lips all around, inevitably — go on for several minutes. The Australian and the Omani fill the room with the infectious warmth of their homelands. After doing her very best to knock both Sarah and me off our feet more than once, Alyssia finally takes a step beyond the entrance hallway. She gives a low whistle.

"Jesus Christ, Emma! I know you said you were earning well, but I wasn't quite expecting a fucking palace!"

Sarah laughs. "She's been pretty restrained, actually. She could have bought the Taj Mahal I think! Hey, come look at this view!"

115

Even Latifa is lost for words as she contemplates the outlook over the Thames and London's most famous landmark, and then the endless urban skyline beyond. "Oh my," she murmurs. "Oh my, oh my, oh *my…*"

She shakes her head gently and looks at me. "I'm so happy for you, girl! Look how quickly things have changed in a few weeks for you. Not so long ago you had to share a bedroom with that blonde scorpion!"

We all chuckle at the memory of me rooming with Petra, which seems a lifetime ago. Then I hear a shriek from the bathroom. Alyssia's obviously slipped in and spotted my epic tub.

"Holy shit, ladies!" We follow the sound to its breathless source. "We are *so* getting naked and sipping champagne in this! I'm having you officially evicted if we don't!"

"Something told me you were going to say something like that in the first three minutes," I grin. "Well, we'll be popping the bath's virginity I guess. I've only been moved in three hours, after all!"

"I think it'll take the four of us," chimes in Sarah. "But it'll be real cosy."

"Even better," purrs Latifa.

Clearly this is going to happen, whether I like it or not.

"And the champagne is on the way," adds Sarah. "My treat!"

As if on cue, the door buzzer sings. Sarah goes to push the button, but before she does, she beckons us over excitedly. We crowd around the little screen above the intercom, which reveals a cute, dark-haired delivery boy waiting downstairs. He's barely into his twenties, and there's a cheeky look about him.

Before I can do anything to stop her, Latifa presses the talk button and puts on her most seductive voice. "Come on up, sweetie. And feel free to take off your shirt."

Latifa is incorrigible! I put my hands over my mouth, but behind them I'm smiling. I can't believe she just said that! There's never a dull moment with that girl around. I wait nervously with the others in the hallway, curious to see what will happen.

A minute goes by, and then he's at our door. He's bearing two enormous magnums of Dom Pérignon. Woah, this looks dangerous. He didn't take the shirt thing seriously, of course. But there's a youthful glow in his cheeks and the kind of smile on his face that says we've just made his day.

It's Latifa who opens up the door. With the rest of us crowded into the corridor not far behind her, we must make an intimidating sight for the poor guy.

"Those look so heavy, babe!" she coos. "Don't you feel like coming in and being our butler? Fancy serving four ladies while they enjoy the best bathtub in London?"

We giggle, his grin turns to a gape, and Latifa ploughs on.

"You'd *have* to lose the shirt, though!"

The poor boy doesn't know what to say or do. He probably thinks he's being teased right now. But then he doesn't know Latifa. I'd say at least half of her isn't kidding. And I can't kid myself either: the thought of the picture she's painting is making a warm feeling develop some place beneath my belly button.

"She's not joking," says Alyssia helpfully. The strong Perth girl steps forward and relieves him of the bottles with a heave. I watch in fascination as his eyes drop to the ample cleavage she's left on display for her journey to London. She holds one bottle in each hand, cocks her head with an air of theatre, raises her eyebrows questioningly, and lets the invitation sink in.

These crazy girls! They haven't even been here ten minutes, and already we're on the verge of something mad.

There's an awkward silence, and I worry that he's going to crumble into a pool of melted nerves, or run for his life. Poor boy. He looks so sweet and innocent, especially facing up to this brazen pair!

But when he opens his mouth, his voice is surprisingly steady. It's also much deeper than I expect for a guy with such spritely features. I wonder if he has a few years of smoking under his belt. Whatever, there's no trace of nerves when he speaks.

"Ladies, it would be my pleasure," he says, making sure to look each of us in the eye, one by one. His confidence definitely has an effect on me. You can sense our awe filling the entrance hall. Suddenly he's the one who owns this scene. "But I've only just started my shift, and I can't just take off. I don't finish until eight. It's only my third day on the job, after all!"

I glance across at Sarah and make big, wide-awake eyes at her. I'm dying to know what's going to happen next in this game they're playing.

"Why don't you girls put those bottles on ice and we pick this up a few hours later?" he suggests forcefully. "You really don't want to drink them now, trust me. They've been in the back of my van all morning. So take my number, and call me after eight."

Wow. He totally took her up on it. And I bet she won't back down on what she's started. I feel a flush of excitement and thank myself for having the good sense to take the three days off while our friends are visiting. I'm already thinking this night could get out of hand — and it's only lunch time!

The air is heavy with sex. And it's not just because of the attractive guy at the door. I sense something big is coming between the four of us. Now that we're away from the weird environment of the school and I've lightened up considerably, things might get pretty wild. After all, the tension has been building pretty much from the day that Latifa and Alyssia spread sun lotion over my naked body at the poolside. I was just never able to let go quite the way they surely wanted me to. And, for all their wicked ways, they never pushed me. Then I got distracted by Sarah.

Now, though, I'm feeling a definite twitch in my leg, and I'm playing with my hair. Sure signs.

Alyssia, meanwhile, is being the practical one and punching his number into her phone. Turns out his name is Scott. She rings his device once. His ring tone is one that gets the others dancing, but I don't even know it. I'm a couple of years the senior of these student types, I suppose. I close my eyes, trying to stop my thoughts running away with me. My God, I am just going to be so horny by tonight. Unless…

"Can't wait, gorgeous," calls Latifa, interrupting my little reverie. He's walking away now, giving us a glimpse of a nicely sculpted ass just before the door shuts. Latifa closes it, turns around and licks her lips.

"Oh God, you two!" I say with a shake of my head. "Okay, whatever happens…don't wreck my new place, okay?" Moving in was painless since I paid a couple of burly guys with a van to take care of all the carrying, and I don't want anything to go wrong now. I had half a mind to enlist the others to help me get all the boxes unpacked this afternoon, before heading out in the evening. But I can tell that's not going to happen.

Latifa, with barely a thought to the bags strewn across the entrance area, claps her hands and calls us to attention. "Right, now *there's* something to look forward to, eh ladies? Now I think it's time we partied. This is our reunion, after all, so I hope you're all ready for a bit of wild!"

"But it's only one o'clock 'Tifa!" laughs Sarah.

"Well, it's seven o'clock in Perth," chimes Alyssia firmly. "So it's easily beer time where I come from. None of us have anywhere to be today, right? No? So…lunch and booze it is. Nothing like an early start."

"We haven't ever gotten wasted together before, can you believe it?" Latifa reminds us. "When better to start than on a Tuesday afternoon? We rock, ladies — simple as that!"

Nobody bothers to get changed before we head down to one of my extremely local restaurants. We settle on seafood, and order whatever we want. Between my credit card and that of Alyssia's dad, there's plenty of money around the table. What's more, I sense we feel no real need to smarten up.

I mean, I don't need to go looking for men right now. Nor do I need to bitchily try to outdo the other women here. There are more than enough posers in this part of London, but I feel wonderfully content with myself. After all, men want me enough to pay a lot of money for me.

And as for edging the other females in the vicinity, I'm not like that. And anyway, the quiet knowledge that I'm so in demand is more than enough for me. That, and the fact that I'm certain that all four of us — and most women, in fact — can easily do what I do. If there were any sense of bitchy superiority in me, it would probably come from knowing that I'm one of the rare ones brave enough to choose the path I've chosen. It's a great feeling, and the best part about it is that I don't need makeup or heels to feel it. It comes with me everywhere I go; a cloak of confidence that I hope will never become a cloak of smugness.

Mussels in white wine sauce kick off proceedings, and our excited visitors have finally managed to calm down to the point where we can quiz them on their plans beyond this afternoon.

Alyssia's been back at her working holiday job serving drinks in a Newcastle nightclub, which is where she first met Latifa of course. She's a little bored of that now, though, and misses her mates back home. Especially now winter is here. She's definitely keen to start selling her body; it's just a question of whether she heads back to Australia or gives London a go.

"Do they have agents like Lucy in Australia?" I ask.

She shrugs. "Dunno. There's probably not quite so many millionaires, I guess. Money isn't everything. But on the other hand, your life here seems pretty fun. I don't know if Aussie men have as much imagination as they've got over here, so maybe I just do a Miss Ridgewell and hit it hard for one or two years before retiring back home? I've got a couple left on the visa."

Like Latifa, Alyssia used an agent who set them up with their place at the school for a small charge. There's no other way, since direct dealing with the school is impossible. Unlike me with my sponsor Charles, they paid their own fees. So, no obligations to the agent. Still, they'd both be likely to slot into work easily enough if they wanted to.

"Remember we made a deal that time you were using the bath in our room?" laughs Latifa with that distinctive cackle of hers. "We said we'd definitely all come to London and we'd all join the same agency! But I've got my studies to finish first, and it wouldn't really be fair to have made you wait!"

"We didn't know much, did we?" I giggle. "Judging by the trouble Sarah's having, we couldn't necessarily all just slot in with Lucy either. She's so picky, and hardly ever takes new girls."

"I think we *could* get in with Julia, the agent who set us up, though," says Alyssia. "We've had a few calls from her. Not pushy ones, really, but…word of our chemistry together seems to have gotten around just a little."

My mind goes back to my chat with Miss Jackson, and I wonder just how much word has gotten around, and about what. Everyone knows everyone in this game, didn't she say?

Latifa's situation is a little more complicated. She needs to stay in the UK — specifically Newcastle — until May, when she'll complete her degree. After that, she's still quite set on going back to work in Oman. Apparently with the full knowledge and support of her parents. I shake my head slowly when I hear this. I'm almost not surprised. I'm more jealous than anything, that her family can be so open.

She's free to spend time in London fairly often between now and then, but she couldn't sign up to an agency. She'll be visiting me again, that's for sure, but she says she's in no hurry to get started working. It's not like money's an issue for her. It's the same for Alyssia, really. Their families are both loaded, and the girls are both ultimately just enjoying life over here. As they will wherever they go.

I do wonder if that agent Julia would take Alyssia without her partner in crime. On her own, she's got tons of great attitude and a heap of skill, but perhaps not quite the airbrushed, feminine look most guys want. She resolves to go and see the agent before getting on a train back up north. I tell her she's welcome to stay at mine, although part of me wonders what I'm getting into. Sarah's cool and lovely, but even one half of Latifa and Alyssia on a long-term basis would make both my brain and my ears hurt.

Sarah tells the others of her plans to sign up to the app Miss Jackson showed me, and they're predictably excited for her. Sorting her profile out is on the list for tomorrow. One way or another, it looks like we're all going places.

The world's longest lunch ends around five, which means we can start going to bars. We switch from white wine to cocktails, ordering drinks I've never considered in places I'd never have stepped in before. Money really does change a few things in life!

The clientele in most of these places is a post-work crowd from the city. It is Tuesday, after all. These people are a lot smarter than we are, and I get that same vibe I got from the property agents. We look so young and casual that we could easily feel out of place. And some people clearly think we are.

But I really don't need to care about that. And it's fantastic that I don't *need* to fit in anymore. It's a wonderful feeling.

Because I know that, if I felt like it, I could make any of the men here grovel before me and pay for the privilege. And if the women give me sneering looks, then I just smile to myself, remembering that the joke's on them.

"You know, they spend their lives checking email and going to meetings, trying desperately to show how they can get ahead in a man's world," I murmur to the girls after Sarah spots one particular female in a grey suit give us a disdainful look.

"And you earn twice as much in a day just for sucking a cock or two!" grins Latifa, pretty much finishing my sentence for me. With all the subtlety of a hammerhead shark, as usual.

"It's quite fun watching them make fools of themselves," I add. "Sitting here knowing what power I've got. Hell, any of those banker guys in expensive suits could be a client of mine. It's a pretty awesome feeling."

"Not so worried about meeting a client in public any more,

then?" Sarah teases, knowing not to say anything about Spurring. She's the only one I've shared all my fears with.

"Maybe I'm getting there," I say thoughtfully, wondering if it's just the cocktails that are letting me ruminate on the idea of crossing paths with a client without having a heart attack.

Although it does suddenly hit me that I'm only living a couple of underground stops away from my last job now. And Spurring. And *her*.

"Let's not talk about work, okay?" I suggest. "We're getting drunk, aren't we?"

"Cheers to that," says Alyssia, as we clink glasses for about the ninth time of the day.

My head's spinning as we trip towards a large nightclub in Piccadilly Circus. We've gotten tired of wine bars and are now fresh from a couple of rounds in some more down-to-earth traditional English pubs. Now we're all in the mood for a dance, and the fact that it's Tuesday really isn't going to stop us if we can help it.

This is turning into a proper girly night out! I'm almost ashamed I haven't properly let off steam like this since getting back from training. We're pushing and shoving and giggling and stumbling down London's (thankfully wide) sidewalks, and I can't think of any people I'd rather share this evening with. These are my girls! And it's so much better with no mentors or wakers or butlers around. We can really be ourselves at last.

"No boys, okay?" slurs Latifa unexpectedly. "This is *our* night, and we stick together. Dance or bust. If any boys come along, you have to share them. Deal?"

We cheer our approval. I certainly don't feel the need to chase men just at the moment, although we're getting our fair share of wolf whistles and chat-ups now. Especially the glamorous Latifa, whose mixed blood and exotic look seem to entrance men from every walk of life. But I feel like I'm worth way more than a whistle and a lame line now. *Way* more.

Oddly, perhaps getting paid for what I do has done wonders for my sense of worth. I haven't really thought much about whether I want to date or have a relationship yet, beyond what's developed with Sarah, which just kind of happened by accident. Between Charles and all the rest of them, I feel like my needs are taken care of without commitment getting in the way.

The air has chilled to a biting, frosty crisp, but the bouncers take no pity on the four shivering girls as they turn us away because I'm wearing sneakers and Sarah's in her most ragged pair of jeans. Pricks! Latifa shouts at them, but even she can't win these humourless oafs over.

We need to find somewhere desperate enough for custom on this, the quietest night of the week. We wander into Soho, and eventually find the kind of seedy bar where I'm entirely confident I'd never meet one of my clients. It has a dance floor around the back, and that's all that matters.

We have it almost to ourselves, but the vibe is surprisingly good. It's hot and sweaty, despite the cooling of the seasons. The heating's up, and I feel my own warmth rise as our drinks count hits the teens. It's gin and tonic all around now — phew!

"How fucked up is it that we end up in a place like this!" shouts Alyssia. "We've got all those £500 dresses from school!"

We all laugh. I blame Latifa for rushing us to get out of the flat and on to the alcohol.

"I'd love to have seen you in an evening gown at lunch time!" comes her retort. She's still surprisingly sharp and switched-on for this time of the evening. We dance for a couple of hours longer, and I'm actually glad of my sneakers. I just want to twist around the dance floor, after all. I'm not here to feel sexy. I can do that any day of the week — and usually do.

The last song is a slow one, and inevitably Sarah pulls me close. We kiss, long and deep, and I don't care that a few boys appear to watch. All of a sudden there are more people in here than I thought — word travels fast I guess.

Over Sarah's shoulder I notice Latifa and Alyssia locked in a similar embrace. Fuck, life is good! I'm just so happy for us all.

It's past two in the morning when they shut the doors on us. Alyssia pulls out her phone for the first time in hours. "Oh God! A call from Scott! *Shit!* We forgot all about him, didn't we?"

"Too much alcohol," murmurs Sarah, leaning against the wall and closing her eyes. "But he'll come. He'll still come."

One thing the delay has done is extinguish any doubts about going through with it. We're fuelled with passion now, after our slow-dance kissing. Endorphins are knocking against my skin in the oddest places, and I'm sure it's the same for the others. We want each other bad now, and a fresh-faced young man would be a cherry on top.

"Yeah, like I said, it's okay if we share," grins Latifa. "We need to take this night to the next level."

I find myself nodding. "Ah, what the heck…tomorrow's a write-off already. Call him, Liss!"

"He's probably gone to bed," laughs the drunken Sarah, entirely contradicting herself as she tries to wave down a taxi.

"Well, if he has, he'll get out of bed for us," declares Alyssia. "I know I would if I were him!"

She proves right. He's still up. And he's coming to pick up where he left off at my new flat. Eek!

"We did remember to put the champagne on ice, right?" asks Sarah.

"Yep, done," smiles Latifa toothily. "We're all set."

There's a nervous lump in my throat and a fire in my belly as we climb into a taxi bound for my apartment.

XV

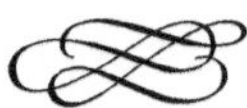

$\mathscr{O}$kay, seriously. Life is so fucking sweet right now, I don't have words for it. I throw my head back, close my eyes and give a funny little growl from the back of my throat as I wallow in decadence. And steaming bath water.

The warm liquid is up to my nipples and London's twinkling lights stretch out before me like it's my kingdom. Maybe it's because I'm so drunk, but the weird window-bath is nothing but brilliant right now. I'm sandwiched between Sarah and Latifa, rubbing shoulders and hips and legs with them as the four of us all squeeze up along one side of the tub to enjoy the magic view.

It's somewhere after 2am, but I'm in heaven. Because I don't have to be anywhere tomorrow, and because I'm with my favourite girls, and because I'm full of booze, and because this wonderful bath is *mine*.

And that's not all. Fizzy champagne — the *real* stuff — is being poured out for us by the most adorable young man. Black jeans, white t-shirt, and a confident way with a heavy bottle. If there's anything to complain about — which hardly seems right — it's that

126

he has to stand behind us, by virtue of the bath stretching right across the room.

But, strangely, we can see his shimmering reflection in the glass window in front of us. Maybe the shimmering is just my intoxicated eyes, who knows. How can you see out but also see a reflection? Then again, who cares? I hold up a hand for my glass.

And who cares that he watched us all get undressed, and probably doesn't know any of our names, and that I'm supposed to be a responsible tenant who doesn't invite intriguing and gorgeous young delivery boys into her apartment?

"Tifa...Tifa..." I slur, whipping my head in the direction of her emerald green eyes, "You...you're so clever. Fuck me, you're clever. We've got this guy here...hmmm...thanks to you..."

My neck lolls forward and I know I'm far gone. Yet I'm definitely horny. I go back to eyeing the reflection, which is now giving Latifa her glass. Oh my, there's an inevitability about this.

Latifa squeezes my leg with her right hand, takes the glass with her left, and turns around to talk to Scott. Oh, she's drunk — but she's very much still with it.

"Hey, didn't we have a deal?" she says to Scott, a touch of acid in her voice.

He looks faintly amused. If I were sober, I think I'd be admiring his restraint right now. I mean, four naked girls in a bath, all to himself. Correction: four *drunk* naked girls in a bath. That's got to be every guy's wet dream right there.

"Did we now?"

Latifa rolls her eyes. "*Yes!* How many times do I have to ask you to take off your shirt?

He says nothing. I just see the reflection put the bottle down on the massive sink area to his right, grab the bottom hem of the t-shirt and heave it over his head. My eyes widen despite myself. Fuck, this guy has been in the gym. A *lot*. Either that, or carrying champagne magnums around London does wonders for the upper body.

Then I notice the tattooed sleeves. My God, the tribal artwork starts halfway up his bicep, runs up to his ox-like shoulders and down the other. This is the kind of thing I don't see on my everyday clients. It's a pleasing change, even if I have no idea exactly what the theme is. Looks Polynesian, maybe. Even though he's clearly a Surrey boy through and through.

We exchange glances and giggles with each other's reflections, and Alyssia simply says, "Oh, yummy."

"Hmmmmnnnn," I smile, leaning back again and closing my eyes, making do with the vision of him that's etched into my mind. Truth be told, I don't think I can really drink this stuff. It's more the decadence of it than really needing a drink. I've got other things on my mind right now. I'm not sure if I've got the energy to act on what's happening in my head, but some deep, alcohol-proof part of my being knows I'm not getting much choice.

Yep, sure enough, there it is. Latifa's hand is back on my thigh. Sarah's is on my other thigh. Instead of tightening, as once I might have, I relax even more. It's sort of like that time at the poolside, except I feel better. Different. I feel like I'm *me*, even as their hands get closer to my pussy — which is now wet in more ways than one.

We're underneath a mountain of bubbles. He won't necessarily know what we're up to in here.

"Oh, *fuck* yes!"

Okay, he knows now. Alyssia, inevitably, has squealed first, presumably because Sarah's right hand is doing the same thing as her left one.

Giggles all round.

Scott sits down on the broad ledge of the bath behind us. He isn't stupid. He knows what's happening beneath those suds.

"Before you get otherwise occupied, ladies, I just want to say thanks for having me here. It's an honour to be butler to four such perfect women, in such a magnificent home.

"Now, do you really want those glasses or shall I free up your hands?"

"Good boy," drawls Alyssia, waving her half-empty glass above her head. We all follow suit, and watch his stomach muscles tighten as he stands and then reaches across for our glasses. My heat's rising as I feel fingers enter me. I know someone's going to bow to the inevitable any moment now.

Someone says: "Oh, shut up and get in the water with us, will you?"

I'm a little surprised to find that that someone is me. But I'm too far gone down the road of pleasure for old Emma to get a look in tonight. And I think the girls are proud of me, judging by the loud murmurs of approval. And by the deep, beautiful kiss Latifa gives me. I'm vaguely aware of Sarah turning her sweet lips to Alyssia. Oh, that's so deliciously naughty. Partner-swapping.

Sort of, but not really. I mean, Sarah's hand is still probing gently between my legs. And I *think* Latifa's hand is guiding it, with the added twist that she's slipping a finger between Sarah's, and straight between my lips. It's my best guess, anyway. All I know is there's some kind of octopus gym routine thing going on down there.

There's a cough behind us, and we all disengage and stare. *Jesus!* His lower half is *not* a disappointment. That muscular V leads to exactly the kind of honeypot a girl wants. It's shaved clean, it's substantial and it's standing very much to attention. I think there are some legs there, too, but my eyes can't get past his cock.

"Well, since you asked so nicely," he grins. And promptly steps right between Sarah and I, as gracefully as the odd and rather packed tub will allow, and sinks to his knees on the other side. His back is to the window and he's facing us. He's tall enough that this keeps his magnificent manhood above the water line. "I'm not sure there's space for me to sink down," he says with mock guilt.

Even the finger in my pussy has stopped wiggling. I think Latifa is actually thrown by what she's seeing. But not for long.

"Hang on! Girls, I think we can forget the London view for a moment. We've got a better one, don't you think?"

Alyssia and Sarah agree enthusiastically, and I give my answer by reaching out and touching it. I'm gentle at first, but then my lust floors me and I begin to massage the balls with pleasing ferocity. He groans and puts his hands behind his head.

The fingers leave my pussy, because they know I want to swim across to him. I do just that, and a moment later he is filling my mouth. I want to cram as much of him in as I can, and I suck on him just like I sucked on that boiled sweet back at school. Only this is both bigger and better than a boiled sweet. So much better.

I cup the balls and let my tongue roam all around and over the tip, simply revelling in the taste. I'm dimly aware that I'm not working right now, but also that it doesn't make much difference. It's ingrained into me that my pleasure will be his pleasure. That mantra has been working for me every time. Pay or no pay.

And just when I move my hands around to grip his firm buttocks and pull him further into my mouth, there are fingers back in my pussy. I'm kneeling, but Alyssia has gotten one of her hands in front of and underneath me while I work. While she thrusts, grazing my clit with her hooked finger, someone else is rubbing my ass and kissing my neck. Fingers tweak each of my nipples hard.

No amount of alcohol could dim a turn-on as blazing as this one. Even though I am cock-worshiping, I feel worshiped. Every single sexual zone in my body is being touched, and the feeling is insane, beautiful, unspeakable.

I feel a need for a kiss, in spite of everything. As if on cue, Scott tells us he's close. I pull my mouth off him, and bring a hand back around to work him to climax. My growing experience — and his growing girth — tells me it won't be more than twenty seconds. I turn to my girl, my main girl Sarah, and begin to kiss her with passion. I'm going to love this, but it's also going to make him explode as I gather pace with my hand.

"I'm there, I'm there," he says tremulously, "Where do you want it?"

Sarah comes off my mouth and presses up next to my cheek. I get what she wants. Some of what I want. Still the touches rain down on my breasts and anus and pussy while I aim him at our two open mouths as best I can.

We are both treated to spurts of his hot, white cum on our tongues. We look at each other before swallowing, look up at him, with his dazed, supremely satisfied smile, then look back at each other. Of course we will.

Sarah and I kiss again, spreading his cream further into each other's mouths, our tongues wrestling in the pearly liquid until it eventually dissolves to a pleasant, salty aftertaste.

Before I know it, things have gotten even more out of control. Scott is a tireless stallion, and what feels like hours pass in the bath. We discover many uses for the ledges to the side of my huge tub, and when I lick Latifa to climax the passion is insane. I finally realise that, deep down, I've been wanting to get my tongue on that exotic pussy ever since that hot summer day by the Cranleigh House pool. It sends an earthquake through my nerves to feel her come.

But even then we're nowhere done. Somehow — I think Alyssia has a lot to do with it — we all tumble out of the bath and pin the willing and relentlessly hard Scott to the heated, slippery tiles. And the four of us proceed to have our way with him like a pack of young cougars on heat.

We tear into the guy as one, each of us taking our own piece of his body. While one of us rides his monumental shaft, another sits on his face and enjoys that searching tongue of his. Another squeezes in to slurp and taste beneath his balls, and the last of us guides his deft fingers into her buzzing pussy.

And yes, each of us takes a turn doing everything. We may be depraved and drunk, but we're completely and utterly fair.

It's something like five thirty when Scott staggers out of the door, finally milked of every drop of spunk he has, and we barely have the strength to kiss him goodbye as we collapse in a naked heap on my gigantic bed.

Oh boy. The pleasure bar has just been raised.

XVI

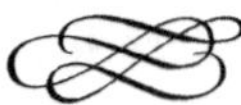

Many hours later, the four of us are back in that tub of mine. It turns out that this amazing place is not only ideal for getting carried away with your friends and a random delivery boy. It's also the perfect place to steam out a howling hangover. It's another sunny day, so it's shades all around for our delicate eyes as we face up to the best window in London. It feels more and more like I've somehow got my own private beach way up on top of an eleven-storey apartment block. Life is getting no less surreal.

It's nearly four in the afternoon. We've managed to keep down the fry-up we ordered from a clever new place that does full English breakfast delivery. Thankfully there's nothing cute about the delivery guy this time. I genuinely don't think any of us could fuck anything today. Our communication has been limited to little more than groans.

But we're starting to perk up at last. Latifa's the first one to attempt any kind of intelligent conversation.

"So, Miss Carling," she says after taking a deep breath. "We need to talk about this business with that guy. Your ex-boss."

I glance at Sarah. I thought we'd agreed not to mention anything

132

about that to anyone. She shrugs. "Er, you spilled the beans very late last night, Em…you were so gone…"

I sigh and shake my head. Alcohol. There's always a downside.

"Oh, right," I say dispiritedly. My head hurts a little too much to have strong feelings about this right now. Trust Latifa to be recovering already. And I bet she isn't going to let this go. Not one bit.

"You can't go on with it like this," she says firmly. "Why won't you tell Lucy? She's always there for you, from what I hear."

I make a face, mainly because I don't really know the answer to that question. But then Sarah leaps into the conversation.

"I think I know the answer to that," she says sagely. "And we may as well talk about this. We're all pretty close now, I think it's fair to say."

The others nod in agreement, and I shrug. Part of me wants to confront this little niggle in my mind with exactly this kind of conversation, but another part still wants to avoid the issue. Especially on a write-off day like this one.

"Let's sort this out, and then we'll get out of the bath and watch a chick flick, okay?" smiles Latifa.

"Fine," I say. "If you know how to sort it out, I'll be pleased to hear it."

"So, as I was saying," resumes Sarah. "I think this has gotten personal with you. You've got your stubborn side, Em, I think we all know that. Deep down you want to tackle this yourself and not give in to this guy. You think complaining and having him taken off your client list will make him a winner, and your pride doesn't want that. Not after the way things ended when you left his company.

"Also, part of you also wants to be the tough girl, doesn't she? I know you're proud of your pain threshold and I'm guessing that deep down you feel the same way about your threshold for mental pain. The whole thing is not only a challenge, but — although it's really scary and threatening — it makes you wet, doesn't it?"

I sigh again. Sarah's managed to order my emotions for me and hit the nail square on the head. Damn, she's gotten to know me far too well.

And I'm hearing murmurs of agreement from the other two. Okay then. So what now?

I cough. "Okay, maybe — so what's the big idea? Get over it and tell Lucy?"

Latifa smiles. "Alyssia and I came up with a more fun idea while we were staggering around London last night. If you want to actually lose this guy without losing face, you only need to get some real dirt on him."

"You're halfway there, I mean, with knowing what you know about his lifestyle," adds Alyssia. "He would never dare fire unless you did first and he had nothing to lose."

"Still, something far more concrete is definitely better," says Alyssia. "Spreading rumours can only be so believable, but nobody could argue with a picture. He'd have to respect it if you had one of those."

"You think I should get a photo and then blackmail him?" I ask incredulously. "I might still be half-drunk, but even I can see that's not going to work out. For about a million reasons I can think of. And Lucy would fire me on the spot."

"Whoah," says Latifa, rolling her eyes. "Back up a second. Not like that, obviously! We were thinking we could help you out. It could be a little group mission to end this bad business. It'll be awesome fun. Sort of like Wicked Witches meet Robin Hood."

"So...you actually want to get this guy ruined?"

"Problem?" asks Sarah pointedly.

"Well," I pause. It's not the worst crusade to embark on, I suppose. The guy is bad to the core. Assuming this mystery client really is him, he's made me horribly uncomfortable. And maliciously so. And I happen to know that he and his management are still making work life very unhappy for some of my friends who are still at the company. Ruining him would be for a greater good. "Yeah, maybe not. But it couldn't be *me* doing it. It's Lucy's business and she'd kill me."

"That's why we have a cunning plan, Emma," grins Latifa again. I can almost see the deviance in her eyes — and she's wearing sunglasses. "This will be a team effort, but it starts with you winning his trust. You need to get him to drop his guard."

"What, really?"

"Yep, really. Your job is to thrive when you're around him. Show him the part of you that's turned on by his attempts to dominate you. Even the threatening part of that, if you can. You've got to get him talking."

"I'm not sure I'm allowed to talk," I say. "He is the customer, after all."

"Nonsense," puffs Latifa. "When a man is turned on and thinks he has *you* turned on, then he's putty in your hands. You can do whatever you like. When you get to that stage, you need to talk dirty to him. If you're clever about it, you'll find out the most disgusting things he's into.

"You've got to play a slow game. And you can: we all know he'd be a fool to really out you like he says he will. He's got way more to lose. It's all talk. So play along; you've got time. Never let on you have the slightest clue who he is. He thinks you're stupid and his dumb blindfold has you fooled. Make out you'll do anything for his silence, and show that you're actually quite liking the things he's doing to you.

"The power exchange will be starting to flow the other way, but he won't feel it happening. He won't have a clue. By showing enthusiasm, you're working towards finding out something he likes doing but that he absolutely wouldn't want photographed. Imagine a big-cheese London CEO getting fucked by a girl with a strap-on, that kind of thing."

"That'd be gold!" enthuses Alyssia. "I'd volunteer to do the fucking. The guy's an asshole and deserves a dildo in his."

"Right," says Latifa. "And Alyssia isn't kidding. This is where we come in. When the time is right, and you've found out a kink like that, you drop hints you know a pair of other prostitutes who are *really* good at that. Ones you went to school with — he'll like that. He won't think you know he was the guy who visited you at the school, will he? He'll just puff up with the secret knowledge he thinks he has. He'll also try to go out and book those girls right away.

"And if he wants you to join this little kink party, you tell him you're not allowed to because those girls aren't from your agency. You'll have to rule yourself out. You're ever so sorry."

She makes a face that says I won't be sorry at all.

I'm beginning to see their plan take shape, and frown as the picture forms in my mind. "And those girls would be…you guys?"

"Me and Alyssia," says Sarah. "Latifa will probably be back in Newcastle, but I'm signing up on that app, aren't I? Alyssia can do the same; or she'll be in an agency. We'll work it out. I just know I'd love to do something big for you, Emma. You've been so good to me. I'd simply love to take that picture while he's got a blindfold on. It would be my pleasure, in so many ways. It's another reason I really like this plan."

"And you'd really have nothing to do with it," adds Latifa. "Not that anything would be said anyway. One tweet from a fake account should do it. Job done."

I must say that there's a lot to like about the plan. Everyone's telling me I don't really need to panic about being 'outed', and with every day that goes by I'm a little bit less convinced 'outing' would be as disastrous as I fear anyway. It doesn't seem like there's a lot to lose, although I'm not so sure my involvement won't be quite easily traceable. Lucy's a sharp cookie.

"Yeah, I see. You're onto something I guess. I just…I think it would come back to me. It wouldn't be hard to work out, would it? He'd make the connection if he knows you're my school friends and something bad comes out of that encounter. Then it would get back to Lucy and the community, and –"

"Small details, Carling, small details!" says Latifa airily. "We'll iron out the business of covering tracks later. Don't worry just yet. It can't do any harm to work towards getting the picture, can it? Once we have it, we can think long and hard about how to use it."

"I suppose so," I say doubtfully. But maybe I'm a little more sold than I believe I am. I especially like the part about enjoying my visits there a little more. I can go with that. Maybe by the time the project nears completion, I'll have decided the guy is nothing but harmless bluster. Or I'll have told the world what I do anyway.

"Cheers to that!" says Alyssia.

Instinctively we look around for our champagne glasses. Then we all start laughing. Because we've made sure to keep booze a long way away from our hurting bodies today.

"Great," says Latifa. "Liss, you're going to see the agency tomorrow morning, and then Emma and I will be photographing both of you to get your app profiles up and running."

I didn't know I was much of a photographer. But I close my eyes, sink down in the water and go with the idea. When Latifa's around, I always have this sense that things are somehow going to work out.

XVII

The next time I go to the mystery house, I'm led along what feels like a different route. After feeling my feet crunching up what must be a garden path, whichever minion is leading the way guides me through the front door as usual. But then there's no turn to the left. It feels like I'm being taken straight on ahead. A door opens, and I'm given a rough push.

Even from behind my blindfold, I can sense there's no light in here. None whatsoever. It smells stuffy and close. Like the inside of a closet. I stumble as I'm pushed into this black void, and reach out to steady myself. There's a wall close in front of me. This may be a broom cupboard by day, I'm guessing. But it's one tiny prison cell by night.

And I'm not alone in here. I can hear *him* step smartly in behind me. It cannot be anyone else. I hear him breathing deeply beside me, sucking air slowly in through the nose. It's menacing and potent.

The door closes.

It's just me and him. Alone. In a dark, tiny and airless room. *Oh God.*

I want to shrink and cower. My heart thumps loudly as I wonder again if he's going too far with his latest stunt. But I remind myself that Lucy has vetted this man. Whoever he is, he can go close to her lines but not over them — or he'll kiss all the Fulford girls goodbye. She wouldn't put any of us in harm's way.

Fingers curl into the blindfold at the temples, inevitably tightening the fabric so hard against my eyes that it hurts. Then, without a word, he gives it a savage pull down. The blindfold burns over my nose and lands squarely in between my lips.

"Bite it," he breathes.

I do as he asks. I understand that my blindfold has now become my gag.

"Keep it between your teeth," he orders, whispering a little louder. "The only sounds I want to hear from you are whimpers. *Bitch.*"

Every part of my body aches to know who my abuser may be. But it's darker than the darkest night in here. I may as well still have the blindfold on. And he knows it.

And yet there's something more immediately threatening about it all, to know that my eyes have been freed. I have an awareness of his body mass near me. Something between a shadow and a silhouette. Yet the only thing I can say for sure is that he's taller than me. *Much* taller.

One of his hands seizes my ponytail, yanking my head back so that it looks up, helpless and held, to where I guess his face must be. The gag is digging into my cheeks. All I can do is wait for his next move.

"Do as I fucking say now, Emma Carling. Or you'll be sorry."

That weird mix of absolute fear and primal lust invades me as he says these words. I gulp and try to nod, but his grip is so tight that all I can do is make an unearthly sound in the back of my throat. It's half gurgle, half wail.

He pushes my head violently forward again, keeping his tight grip on my hair. The fingers creep up towards the roots now, hurting me in a different way. This man is a master of pain. And he enjoys giving it.

He lets go of my hair and slips the straps of my light dress over my shoulders. The garment falls to the floor. I have been instructed to come in panties only. I fear these are soaking wet, despite myself and my dread, as I stand trembling and topless.

"Hands behind your back," he orders.

There's no way he can see me doing what he commands. But I know he knows I've done exactly what he wants.

He grabs my throat with both hands, wedges his knee into the V of my panties and pushes me so that my back is up against the wall.

I dare not breathe, for wondering what is going to happen next as he relaxes his grip and the shadow takes a small step back from me. There must be a little more room inside here than I thought.

A minute of silence passes. Maybe an hour. Maybe ten seconds. Waiting makes time an irrelevance. Waiting becomes me. My eyes are torn between straining for a clue about him and trying to close.

Slap!

His bare hand on my left breast. Hard.

Slap!

How is his aim so good in the dark? It's violent enough to make my whole body tremble, yet each time it grazes my nipple so that my knees almost give way.

Slap!

"Fucking *whore*, Emma Carling!"

My blood goes cold every time he uses my last name and reminds me of what I'm doing for a living. Sure, I am Emma to every customer. But Lucy swears she never reveals my surname.

Too many brutal slaps rain down on my breasts to worry about it for long. He is mixing and matching now. Both sides are stinging and throbbing in stereo.

And when one breast gets hit, the other isn't quite sure what to think.

The feel of his harsh skin on mine. My nipples on fire as my stomach pushes out, filled with knots of fear. The darkness; the closeness; the imprisonment. *Christ, I want to touch myself.*

At the same time, he is pushing me to the limit. I don't know if I can take many more slaps. Each one feels harder than the last. It's like he wants to crack my willpower.

"What a good little bad girl she is," mocks the voice. "Paid good money to have her tits slapped. What would her mother say if I told her?"

And now I do close my eyes. He's messing with my head, I tell myself. I remind myself of everything my friends and Miss Jackson told me. Even if he really does know my mum, he wouldn't dare. He couldn't.

I'm supposed to be thinking of ways to put Latifa's plan into action.

Slap!

And my mind goes straight back to fuzz. Back to the inky blackness and gushing wetness of the here and the now and his hand.

"Ah, so turned on," he whispers, pausing to run his fingers across the giveaway fabric between my thighs. "Good for nothing but selling herself."

I whimper at the feel of his hand down there, unable to deny what he said about being turned on. But the last part? Nasty. I *hate* him. I hate all these weird fuckers who use prostitutes and then berate us for being sluts. I've heard about twisted men like this.

Maybe it's not Spurring at all. Maybe it's just a random guy who stalked me enough to work out my name, and gets off on verbal abuse.

If only he would raise his voice above a whisper. I'd know if it was Spurring then. Even an accent might be a clue. But you can't hear the accent of a whisperer.

"Ha, you want me to fuck you, don't you?"

I won't answer him. Whatever he might be doing to the flow of moisture between my legs, I hate this nasty fucker. Maybe it's unprofessional, but I don't want to give him the satisfaction. Our big plan is floundering already.

He doesn't like my silence. He slaps me across my breasts again, twice as hard as anything that went before. I squirm, this time from pain as much as anything. The shock to my skin radiates slowly out in languid, powerful waves.

"You can fuck this instead," he says, before plunging his hand into my panties and ripping them in two. "Squat. Don't use your hands."

I do it. I have no clue what to expect.

He is down before I am, doing something beneath me as I lower myself onto my haunches. It's the worst moment of the night. I am terrified by the possibilities. Am I about to feel the sharp prick of a spike? A needle? Something hot, maybe boiling?

But what I feel nuzzling at my lips as I settle into place is familiar plastic. He holds it long enough for it to gain traction in my pussy, then I sense him moving away. I am glad he can't see my face right now.

Only as I really succumb to a natural squatting position and adjust my weight fully do I realise how enormous it is. The dildo must be attached to some kind of stable base, but I can't physically get far down enough to feel that bottom part. It's long enough that I can't use all its length. It's thick as four fingers and I feel utterly filled.

I have never sat on a dildo before. Despite the coercion and the nastiness of my situation, I revel in the feeling it gives me.

He pushes down on my shoulders, making me yelp with pain as the toy touches places I didn't know I had. The fucker. I loathe him. I love it.

"Like that, Emma Carling. Stay like that. Legs open. And you know what? I was kidding. Don't fuck it, after all. Keep still now. Just sit on it, like a good little whore. You can go home unsatisfied tonight."

Shit. Fucking it was just what I was thinking. Although I really don't want to make a show for him. He doesn't deserve it.

So I squat there with my knees splayed, my breasts still burning and a dildo for a seat, awaiting his next move.

After five minutes of silence, though, during which I simply cannot get my brain to think beyond his breathing and the enormous object inside me, he clears his throat.

"I've had enough of you," he growls softly. "When I've gone, you can get the fuck out of my cupboard."

I nod. Stupidly, because he can't actually see me. I remember to whimper something like assent, but not before he slaps me square across the face.

"You'd better not ignore me like that next time," he says in his loudest whisper yet.

Then I hear the door open and slam.

Footsteps recede in the distance. There's a brief silence, and I wonder what I'm supposed to do, alone in the house without a blindfold for the first time. Am I supposed to wait for guidance?

I blush in the dark that my first thought is to start moving my hips above that dildo inside me. He won't know, will he? And my need is so heavy right now.

But just as I begin to find some rhythm after a few strokes, footsteps return outside the door. Lighter ones this time.

I have to stop. Esmeralda enters my little cell, telling me she'll re-attach my blindfold, help me dress and see me out. I get a sense of a slight and slender figure, but it's only a silhouette because the hall lights are off too.

A minute later I'm crunching back down that garden path towards my driver. Blindfolded, frustrated, confused and angry once more.

XVIII

The next few days are hard to keep up with. We have great fun photographing Alyssia and Sarah, and filling their profiles on the hooker app. My living room is a symphony of giggling as we gather around Latifa's phone and fill out all sorts of kinky information that will sell my friends' bodies online. Alyssia goes to see her agent contact, too, and will hang around London for a few days until she gets an answer.

She'll stay at my flat, of course. Once Latifa heads back up north and our little school reunion has come to an end, I'm relieved to discover that Alyssia's a lot quieter when her partner in crime isn't around. Sarah and I just don't give her quite the same energy to feed off. And that's a good thing.

The two of them are busily preparing one of my other bedrooms for the possibility of, er, client entertainment. They've been disappearing off on shopping trips, presumably courtesy of Alyssia's father's credit card, and they won't let me come with them. I think they're trying to build some kind of kink palace in there, and they want to make it a surprise. Deliveries start arriving after a couple of days, but they keep the door shut on their little decoration project.

It's like I've got a crew of little worker elves in my home, like it or not.

Their profiles are both flooded with views, but they haven't hit the 'available' button yet. I guess they need to get the bed set up, or something.

"You're sure this is not going to get me in trouble with the landlord?" I wonder out loud.

"It seems like home visits are common practice," shrugs Alyssia. "I wouldn't worry too much. It's not like there'll be guys going in and out every half an hour. It'd only be temporary for me. And I think we'll be sensible about the volume of callers, won't we Sarah?"

Sarah smiles and nods. "Thanks for being cool about everything," she says, looking a little moist around the eyes. "I feel like my luck's turning, thanks to you. Once the bank balance is sorted I can quickly get my own place — for work purposes at least!"

I'm glad she adds that last bit. My heart skipped a beat when I thought she was suggesting moving out. For all my antics and all my group sex activities, Sarah has become someone I can't live without. I'm probably cool with her working out of the flat next door in the longer term, if she's going to pursue selling her services via the internet, but I like going to sleep in her arms too much to want to give that up.

There's quite the pile of work waiting for me after my few days off. Lucy has been filling up my schedule, and I'm booked in with two clients a day for my first four days back. Coupled with my grooming appointments and medical check-ups, I feel positively rushed off my feet.

"Boo hoo," jokes Sarah when I make mention of the state of my diary. "Only got four hours for lunch now, have we?"

Alyssia guffaws, and I know they're right. You get spoilt pretty quickly in this life. On average it's usually less than four hours across an entire day and evening that I'm busy. I mustn't forget how good I've got it.

Whatever happens, I keep reminding myself, I must not cock things up or cross Lucy. She continues to be constantly on the lookout for my wellbeing. I'm willing to go with the little plan we've cooked up for Spurring, even if I got too distracted to put phase one into action last time around. But part of me thinks I might just end up coming clean with Lucy rather than really going through with the whole thing. We will see when the time comes. Anyway, I need to have another go at winning his confidence before anything too devious can happen.

The sexual adventures come thick, hot and fast. There's my regular night with Charles, who informs me that he's signed me up for that sushi-making course. I had forgotten all about it, but clearly he hadn't. Despite my protests, he's paying for it. He tells me to consider it an early birthday present. It's a couple of weeks until I turn twenty-seven, and he asks if I mind him booking me that night.

I say yes straight away, since I know he's going to make the night as special and romantic for me as any boyfriend ever did. Or ever could. And I can't help thinking I'll get some obscene tip attached to my fees. He knows I won't take his cash any more. I love him to bits.

Though he's not into anything extreme, he's got a subtle imagination. This week he stands me on a little pedestal in front of the full-length mirror in his bathroom. I'm in a short skirt, and soon I can feel the clawing touch of the air beneath it as he stands behind me and pulls my panties down over the shiny black heels he sent me earlier in the day.

He instructs me to part my legs, which I cautiously do, wary of my balance on the stunning new Prada shoes. I needn't worry: he crooks a strong arm around my waist and steadies me as he unzips and slips into me with a hot breath that speaks of his need.

It's amazing watching us, fully clothed, rutting in this unusual position. It should be awkward, but he's prepared everything so that it's not. He keeps his — and our — balance and timing so well that I can throw my arm around his neck behind me and he can caress my blouse-shrouded breasts with his spare hand. I close my eyes, glance in the mirror, and then do it all over again. And I come before he does.

Lucy also sends me on my first 'top' assignment. Instead of me getting some kind of punishment, it's an introduction into the huge and lucrative world of dishing it out. I haven't ventured into that scene since the day I lost the plot with Petra and Rupert, but everyone seems convinced that was some kind of virtuoso display that betrayed a natural aptitude.

I'm not quite so sure of that as I approach the entrance to some prime real estate on Knightsbridge. My heart is beating a little faster than it would for most assignments. I've been told that this is a fairly straightforward 'spank and tickle' assignment and that I should breeze through it. As you might expect, the details are mostly down to my creativity: it's up to me to control things and give him an entertaining ninety minutes. All that's certain is that I should end off by riding him and applying a gentle choking hand around his throat.

Jesus, I don't want to get that last part wrong.

I am shown in by an expressionless butler and waved into a small reception room next to the front door. "You are to change here and then move through into the next room, Madame."

I nod and wait for him to leave. As I'd been warned it would be, my outfit is laid out on the coffee table, alongside a riding crop, a paddle, a belt and something that resembles a feather duster. This room has a couple of armchairs, a few books and a coat railing. It feels like a misguided sort of cloakroom, into which someone might walk at any moment. Getting changed in here seems odd, but after the bizarre scenes I've lived through in last few weeks I barely give it a thought and quickly strip down.

Soon I'm clad in a tight leather corset, black PVC skirt and long black boots that do up with a series of metal buckles from behind. I apply some of the dark makeup that's been left for me, using the mirror behind the door. For the first time in my life, I am wearing black lipstick. I'm quite pleased with my transformation. I don't bother with underwear.

I open the door, look cautiously around it, and let myself into a room that's only slightly bigger than the one I'm leaving. This is central London, after all, and even men who can afford seven hundred and fifty an hour for me don't get much space for their money. There's room enough for a desk, however, and lying on that desk is a man who is clearly expecting me.

As I shut the door behind me, I take in the fact that he's bent over the desk and facing away from the door. He's not young: the top of his head is shiny and bald, and the neat, combed hair around the sides is distinctly grey. He wears a tweed blazer that should probably have been consigned to history a few decades ago, and below that, shorts and long socks. Shiny black shoes complete the picture.

Oh. I see. He's…he wants to be a schoolboy again. Fuck me, that's twisted! I glance at the many books around the room, and the piles of yellowing paper on the computer-free desk, and guess that he must be some kind of academic. Probably a smart man, one who loves books and the English education system. One who needs a little guidance in these modern times.

He's saying nothing, and I sense this is where my creative part starts. I sink straight into my role, finding it surprisingly easy. "Young Master Doncaster, I understand that you've been sent to the head mistress's office. I'm pleased that you've at least managed to be on time and to assume the correct position. I wouldn't want to have to add to your punishment."

He looks around at me with wide eyes and a gaping mouth, then closes them and licks his lips after he drinks me in. "Yes, head-mistress. Thank you, head mistress," he whimpers softly.

I smile to myself and pull the belt slowly between my fingers. All of a sudden, I think this is going to be really easy.

"Where are you ticklish, young man?" I bark. I'm back in that room with Petra and Rupert now. "And don't lie to me, or I will double your punishment."

He pants heavily as he answers. "My…my…I mean…under my arms and…my stomach…and…"

He pauses.

I tap my foot.

"And *what?*" I hiss.

He answers in barely a whisper. "And my penis, head mistress."

"Very well, Master Doncaster," I tell him, picking up the feather duster thing. "Then we'll begin."

The ninety minutes fly by, and as usual I get so carried away that I go a little over time.

That isn't the only new experience Lucy signs me up for in this amazing week. She also has me servicing a couple for the first time. It never crossed my mind I'd ever be doing that. Even after several weeks in the game, I'm still a little naïve at times.

"People *do* that?" I ask incredulously. "Married couples?"

"Of course, Emma!" Lucy laughs down the phone line. "Gosh, I've got several couples on my books, all looking to spice things up. Obviously this is an exception to my 'no married clients' rule. If they're both in it together, then nothing pleases me more than supplying one of my charming ladies.

"Most often it's the woman wanting to explore another woman while the husband watches, or even a full-on threesome. Occasionally the wife likes the idea of watching her husband fuck another woman: although you need to be very aware on those assignments. Sometimes it turns out they're more jealous than they expect to be."

This particular night, though, has an extra twist. It seems Lucy considers very few tasks beyond me, even with so much new stuff going on. This, apparently, is a couple who've done this many times, although they almost never take the same girl twice. The wife wants a female 'pet' for the evening. I will be her plaything, kept on a leash at all times. The husband will mostly watch, but sometimes the wife will let him do things to her pet.

The thought of this particular night out floods my lady parts instantly. Christ, the possibilities!

The call-out itself, in a large apartment not far from my own, certainly doesn't disappoint. The door opens even before I get the chance to ring the bell, and an attractive, blue-eyed blonde in her forties, wearing a figure-hugging red dress, appears. She looks me up and down for a moment, then grabs my elbow and pulls me inside without a word. She hauls me into their living room, where her sophisticated-looking husband sits impassively in a large armchair. He has tanned skin and curly, charcoal hair. His fingers, one of which sports a prominent wedding band, are steepled in front of him as he watches the developing scene with interest.

The woman — she's really gorgeous — silently takes my handbag off my shoulder and tucks it behind the sofa. She turns me to face her husband, and presses up behind my back, placing one hand on my hip. I can't help breathing in sharply as she whispers in my ear, just loud enough for him to hear.

"My pet…*my* pet. Don't speak, just do as you're told. It's time to collar you."

Holy *fuck*, I'm wet.

She strips me, button by button and zip by zip, while her husband looks on. Every so often she stops to smell my hair or breathe hotly on a part of my body. In no time I am naked, my knees are weak and I'm trembling with desire.

"Look at my pet, baby," she says to her man. I'm not sure if I should look at him too. I focus on the middle distance. "Look how perfect she is! Thank you for her."

"It is my pleasure to watch you enjoy her," he says in a well-rehearsed tone. "Collar her and take her in every way."

Wow, there's some serious power dynamics going on here, I think to myself as I feel leather tightening around my throat. So he's the big boss, but he wants to watch her dominate me. And she really, really wants to do that. I'm serving him, through her. Alpha, Beta, Gamma.

Cold metal slithers down my back now. That must be the chain. Holy mother of God, I'm horny now. "Get on your hands and knees, pet," she says in an even tone that doesn't sound like it should be messed with. "We're going for a little walk."

I'll do anything she tells me, and I suspect I'd do it even if I weren't getting paid. She walks me around the apartment, where she has left treasures all over the floor. Treasures like dildos, posters of unbelievably ripped men, and bottles of scented lubricant. She makes me lick them and kiss them with my mouth, but she won't let me touch them.

If she's trying to get me sexually wound up, it's working.

Finally she leads me to her husband, still sitting on the armchair like a king sits on a throne. He's fully dressed, but he parts his knees as I crawl towards him with the chain tugging at my throat.

"Have a sniff, have a lick, pet," purrs the blonde wife. "But as always, don't touch."

I breathe in the scent of expensive tailoring and shoe polish as I follow her instructions, almost fainting with sexual intoxication. My mouth can just about reach his crotch, where I smell raw desire and nuzzle against the bulge in his trousers. Then I turn my neck and look up questioningly at her.

"Very good, pet," she says approvingly. "Have a treat."

She holds out a strawberry in her hand. I take it in my teeth and swallow. My heart keeps on beating faster now. She leads me over to the fireplace and ties one end of the lead to a metal ring on the mantelpiece. I am still on my hands and knees as she moves around behind me.

"Reach behind you and spread your cheeks," she instructs.

I do exactly as I'm asked. I know there's a good chance cream will be dripping from me already. I am glad for their sake that this is a marble floor.

"Oh, there's a cream factory in there, baby!" she says to her husband. "She's so wet! My horny little pet!"

I groan quietly at her oh-so-true words, and my back arches in frustration.

"Face the window," she says quietly.

That means I have to turn so that my ass faces her husband. And as I do so, I can hear her moving towards him. "Drink from the bowl if you are thirsty, pet. No hands."

God, they really have left a bowl of water for me. Fuck, and now that she mentions it, I really am quite parched. The heating is up in here, and I've been crawling around on all fours for a while now. I lean forward and lap up the liquid as best I can. The submissive feeling I get is out of this world.

I hear rustling behind me, and then things go quiet. I am sure nobody has left the room. What's going on? Are they reading? I think they might be, because all I can hear is what sounds like the occasional page turning. It's pure torture, this. I have no idea what's going on behind me. This goes on for something like forty minutes.

Then I start to hear movement. Groans and movement, to be precise. Unmistakeable heavy breathing and groans. "Turn around, pet," she orders.

Oh, they will drive me insane! She's on her husband's lap in the armchair, bent back over his chest while his arm comes around and reaches beneath her skirt. From the noises she's making, I don't have to think too long about where his fingers might be.

They're driving me crazy, and they know it.

She orgasms loudly, though whether it's real or for my benefit I'm not sure. "Did you enjoy that, pet?" she asks with a mean grin.

I nod. But I want more, and she knows it. I begin to pant, and let my tongue hang out like a dog's.

"I think she should get a treat again, baby," she says to her husband. He nods, and the woman in red walks over to me. "Kneel."

I do as she tells me.

"Now taste my pussy, pet. Taste it."

She pulls up her skirt and stands directly above my face. It tastes like absolute fucking honey.

After that, she uses and abuses me in every way imaginable. She fucks me with a strap-on, missionary-style, while I lie on my back and hold my knees in the air. It's kinky as fuck and hotter than hell to have a woman on top of me, breast to breast, while feeling a sensation that's exactly like a man's thrusting.

And we're not nearly done. I lick her to climax twice, she slaps my nipples with a paddle and she takes me for more walks with butt plugs in my ass. The one thing I don't get to do is come.

Finally, with my time nearly up, she leads me to her husband. "Do you like my pet, baby? Do you want to play with her?"

He just smiles. First she tells me to take out his cock and suck it. Like the slut I have become, I was panting for that instruction. Only a tiny part of me, now, is disgraced and ashamed at myself, but I quite like it being there. I've come to learn that it makes the rush wilder for the full-volume turn-on that fills the rest of me at times like this. I don't think I want to lose that little shred of shame I have left.

I feast on him with my hungry mouth for a while, my vagina tingling maddeningly as her fingers tickle the back of my neck, a constant and reassuring touch from the tasty treat's wife; one that reminds me just how delicious this depravity is.

Then a gentle push on my shoulder. "Kneel back on your heels, little pet," she purrs. I uncork him from my mouth to do as she says, and I swear I feel another surge of liquid in my core. Merely from the rush of doing her bidding.

She squats down behind me. Her left hand creeps around and holds me firm by the stomach. Her right takes me by the throat, gently tilting my head back so that when I open my eyes, I see him standing above me, holding his hardness in his hand. The way she holds me; this is what a doll must feel like.

I fucking love it. I could be a doll all day. I'd do it for free.

The way she holds me for him is driving me to a frenzy. It's doing the same thing for him. He seems so tall from here; his dick so menacing. So *promising*. I can see it pulsing larger by the second as he works his own length with rhythm.

He uses his left hand, and I can see the wedding band he wears. *I bring spice to marriages*, I think to myself, and I groan at the thought.

Her hand is dropping down my stomach, one finger so close to my clit. But she won't touch it. It's *his* pleasure I'm being held for now, not my own. The desire hammers away in my skull.

Then his burning seed is on my face, and I shudder at the wanton thrill as the hot drops land. I close my eyes just in time, and the shower hits me on my cheeks, my nose, my upper lip and my chin. My breasts rise and fall with my heavy breath as he empties himself all over me.

His doll. Her pet. Her doll. His pet. I smile.

"Look at her face!" she says. "I knew this one would be something different. Lucy was right."

I'm not sure what she's talking about. The sight of my cum-spattered countenance?

"One in a thousand," he murmurs, and I open my eyes to see him shaking his head in wonder. I'm curious. What did I do? "That smile is worth every penny."

I twig what they're on about. I'm guessing most girls frown or spit or look away when he does what he just did.

Me? I just did what came naturally. I smile when I'm happy.

"God yes," she whispers. "Turn around now, pet."

The best ride I've ever had continues as I face her now, still on my knees, and she licks her husbands' semen off my face. Every last drop of it. She makes little orgasmic noises at every slurp, twirling her tongue slowly on my pulsing skin as she savours the flavour. I respond in kind, because, holy fuck, it's hot what she's doing.

She's done, and she pecks me on the lips. Just as I begin to probe for her tongue, though, she pulls me onto his lap, and tells me to ride him. I go willingly, let him fuck me hard, and thank God I climax when he does.

Nights like these mean I am loving my job more than ever now. There is absolutely no way I can lay this down. I'm almost drunk with the power and the excitement and the money. Lucy must be kept sweet at all costs. I'm getting very, very wary of this plan I've cooked up with the girls.

But it's also getting harder and harder to bottle up what I do. Not only do I know a lot of people whom I suspect (though I bet they wouldn't say it out loud) would be downright jealous, but I feel like I can be proud of my art. Apart from, say, the technicalities of cock-sucking, I'm beginning to see that it's quite something to be able to switch from dom to sub the way I can.

I can't shake the feeling that I'm going to have to tell my mother, sooner or later. I can't hide the fact that I've moved house much longer. She likes to visit me now and then. So, with trepidation in my voice, I phone and invite her to my new place for lunch. There's no way my dad can be there. If I tell her, she can pass on the news. Looking him in the eye will be far too much.

"How can you afford to live *there*, darling?" she asks.

"Oh…I'll explain everything next week, Mum."

I gulp as I put the phone down. I'm either going to have to go through with my confession or come up with one hell of a lie.

XIX

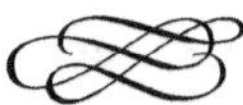

"Is it reversible?" I ask Lucy, wondering if her latest plan is confirmation that she's finally decided to start playing impish jokes on me. I am, after all, now more than three months into my new career.

"Oh, it will have to be," she giggles. "Most clients prefer a pure and natural look. The piercing will be buried in there somewhere, but you won't even be aware of it in the future. That's what the experts are telling me, anyway."

"Nobody has done this before?" I quiz her.

"Not one of my girls," she admits. "But the interesting new requests are exactly what makes this job such a fascination, you know?"

I'm really going to have to think about this. I'm getting the feeling I've become a go-to girl for the clients and for Lucy whenever there's a more 'niche' business enquiry. Word seems to be getting around, and, just as Lucy promised, my fees are creeping up.

"I could have you working all day if I wanted to, young lady! I'm turning down eight out of ten requests for you now, and the waiting list is going out to about a month. You are creating a stir I've never quite seen before."

"Oh…" Is all I can think to say, still quite unable to take in the level of fuss. I almost feel like I've become a celebrity, albeit one that will (I really hope) never appear in a newspaper. "That's amazing, Lucy! Really?"

"Would I lie to you? Emma, you're the hottest property in London right now. I've even heard that you're at the top of certain rankings lists in some very high-security intranet systems."

"They have rankings?" I laugh, more amused by the notion of rankings than the fact that I might be top of the pile.

"Even I'm not privy to these particular networks," Lucy tells me, "but I believe that there are a couple of lists out there for the high net worth individuals that form our client base. Much as they treasure confidentiality, they love to compare notes. And to rate girls for their performance on any number of criteria. I've only been told this verbally mind you, but apparently some of the ratings software has decided you're number one by quite some margin."

I make a mental note to ask Charles about this next time we're together. Which reminds me of something I've been meaning to say to Lucy.

"By the way, you're not turning down requests from Charles, are you?" I ask, trying not to sound too hopeful and give myself away. I think I'd die if our appointments stopped. Would anything stop us from seeing each other outside of 'work'? Only his policy of keeping his sex life the way he does. And, God, he's probably right. If there was even a hint of real-life 'relationship' about it, I'd fall so hard that I'd break every bone in my body.

I'm sure Miss Jackson wouldn't approve of my feelings for Charles, but I think that times have changed since I embarrassed myself with Rupert. My awareness of the dangers of attachment is complete, and I think I know what I'm doing now. Besides, he's the only one of my dozens of clients that has this kind of effect over me, so I think I'm doing all right.

"We all need our little vice, don't we?" chuckles Lucy, echoing my thoughts. I can almost see her beaming down the phone again. "No, as your sponsor and one of my very first clients he will always have special privileges. You'll have your weekly with him as long as you want it."

I'm relieved to hear that. I've been working on the sushi thing, after all, and must say I'm really enjoying it. What a crazy indulgence to be able to go to a course on Japanese raw fish preparation at eleven on a Wednesday morning! This life is opening doors for me in so many more ways than one. No way in a million years would I have found the time or energy to broaden my horizons in that way whilst I had a full-time 'day job.'

"Apart from that, it's about taking the best offers for you, working on roughly two grand an hour as your standard rate. Considerably more for major kink. Then of course there's keeping things interesting for you and making sure long-term clients are prioritised. It's not an easy balancing act, but that is exactly what I am here for, Emma."

I nod, which is silly, because we're on the telephone. She keeps going.

"Anyway, we've gotten right off the subject! A ring in your clitoris, to be worn until Christmas. £25,000 in your bank to cover the inconvenience. And no doubt a few lost bookings."

My world grows ever more bizarre and twisted. I can't quite work out what's more strange: the offer itself, or the fact that I'm considering it.

"Who's it for? What do they want from it?"

I don't know much about clit rings. Such decoration has never been that high on my list, I have to say.

Lucy clears her throat, as if she knows I won't like what I'm about to hear. "It's the one you're not allowed to see. The house in — oops, careful! The place where you get blindfolded."

Although I've not said anything to her whatsoever, I think she senses that part of me loathes this particular client. I suspect she knows me well enough, too, to sense that I am torn apart by the turn-on of going there. And now she can hear me thinking, it seems.

"Emma, if there's anything you want to say about those visits, I'm all ears. We can afford to be a little more choosy these days."

I feel my jaw tightening a little. "Of course I will. I mean, so, he's a long-term client, right?"

"Very," she admits. "But that isn't everything, and you know that. *You* are my priority."

I'm on the verge of saying something. Telling Lucy things is so much like falling into your mother's arms when you've hurt yourself as a child. But then I think of Latifa and the girls, and the plan we cooked up in the bath. They were right; this is something personal and I want to see it through. I'm curious and aroused and fascinated by it all. And I've come to realise that as much as he thinks he's the winner in all this, he's not. He doesn't know I know (or think I know) who he is, and that I can get him if I play my cards right. Plus, I'm taking his money. Way more of it than his stupid company payroll ever used to grudgingly shove my way. There's a weird pleasure in that.

"No, everything's fine," I announce, trying to sound firm about it. "But we're talking about some fairly serious mutilation here. Can we make it fifty thousand?"

Lucy lets out a low whistle. "I like it, Emma Carling. You know what you're worth. I'll ask the question, and I'd be very surprised if it wasn't a yes."

"Thanks Lucy," I smile, feeling apologetic in a British kind of way.

"That little pussy of yours is a gold mine, you know that?"

She chuckles heartily whilst I turn red at her decidedly un-British words. Thank goodness she doesn't ask me to answer her before ringing off.

～

The next day is a busy one. Coffee with an ex-colleague (she's also moved on now, thankfully for her) in the morning, and I'm absolutely dying to tell her what I'm up to and what the loathed but to-die-for boss gets up to in his free time. It's on the tip of my tongue, but I'm not sure I can trust her to keep a secret.

Then I'm off making sushi, which is terrific fun. It feels like I'm back at holiday club. The pleasure of taking time over creating something; learning an art that's genuinely new and decidedly tricky to master. I'm starting to produce some passable creations now, and I can't wait for Charles to eat them off my naked body.

It makes me wet just thinking about it as I stand there mushing cold rice with my fingers, struggling with the seaweed. The rest of the dozen-strong class are mostly older women, seemingly all housewives of richer men looking for something to do. It's an expensive course, enough so to rule out the average Londoner. And besides, most people my age are at work.

As I cut salmon slices I wonder if any of their husbands are frequenting the likes of me via less scrupulous agents. Of course they are. Or maybe — and I like this thought so much more — some of them are spicing up their marriages the way that wonderful and open-minded pair did with me.

A couple of the women ask me what I do, but I just smile and tell them I'm self-employed. One of them, a blonde lady with blue eyes and a really friendly face, keeps on at me for more details. I hate lying and wish she'd drop it. Eventually I cave. Well, just a little.

"All right, all right," I whisper, making sure nobody else can hear me. "I do massage. Freelance…"

I guess I've decided that I don't know a soul here, and these people have no overlap with any of my other circles, so it's probably a safe place to start practising a little honesty.

"Ah," she says, quite obviously in no doubt as to what I mean. She smiles at me and squeezes my arm. "Well, I won't ask you any more questions, I understand! You're beautiful, Emma – I bet you're doing really well for yourself."

She winks and turns back to her work. I'm so relieved. I melt and beam and have to bite my tongue to stop the imp in me piping up with, "Number one in London, since you ask!"

Wow, telling someone wasn't so bad. God, if only my mother can react like that when we meet up in a few days. I think that is entirely wishful thinking, but hey, a girl can dream.

After that I nip home for a shower and to change. Completely free of fish odours that would definitely not be good for my position on these mythical rankings, I dash out for a lunch-time appointment. It's another first for me: I will actually visit an office!

I'm a little nervous about it. Thankfully it's near Liverpool Street and a fair way from my old office, but still, it's broad daylight and a ton of people my age will be working there. Hotels and homes are one thing, but turning up at an office in the middle of the day seems highly risky. Either the clients (yes, there are two of them, but that's no longer the slightest concern to me) don't care, or they have some pretty major privacy measures in place.

I'm glad I've been told I can dress in 'business wear', otherwise I wouldn't have taken the job. It's actually another large consultancy and, if I ran into anyone familiar, I could legitimately say I'm in for an interview.

As it turns out, I don't spot any familiar faces and am treated by security exactly as I would be if I really were in for a job application. Though I know I'll be getting a stern examination of a different kind, I suspect this is exactly what the various gatekeepers have been told. The EA who shows me into the executive's office is either a very good actress or genuinely thinks I'm there for entirely innocent reasons.

Once I'm in, the latch is flicked and two men in their forties greet me with a formal handshake each. "Emma, how lovely to meet you, please have a seat," they say, motioning to a long rectangular table in the corner of the office. They look completely smart and serious, both with a modern business look: fashionable stubble, sharp eyes, gelled hair.

"Thank you," I answer, smoothing down my skirt and straightening my blouse before sitting down. I've not had a lot of clear instruction of what to expect from this assignment, but I'm getting used to just going with it.

They each pull out a chair and sit down opposite me, putting their phones (two each) on silent before placing them on the table. They look a very similar age and stocky build, and I wonder if they were at school together. Maybe even on the same rugby team. There's something a bit old boys' club about the feeling in the room, but at the same time the atmosphere is formal and, well, rather like it really *is* an interview.

At first, I wonder if there's been an enormously embarrassing mix-up. They begin to ask me the most mundane and general interview-style questions I've ever had to deal with. Strengths, motivations, weaknesses, education and all the rest. They don't seem to have an actual CV of mine, but the questions are vague enough that they could apply to any job and any applicant.

As always, I just go with it. Just as I'm beginning to wonder if making me squirm is all they want to do, the one executive whispers in the other's ear. His colleague nods, leans back and taps his pen on the table.

"So far so good, Emma. We feel you may have what it takes to succeed here. However, we hire on looks too."

"That's right," the other one jumps in. "This is not a politically correct company. What we look for, among other things, is highly fuckable women. We are senior board members and we are used to getting what we want. If you work here, we will expect you to open your legs for us any time you are summoned. So then, will you stand up and follow our instructions. Begin by removing your clothing. Lose everything except the shoes."

I see what's going on here now. This is the fantasy for them; the interview they wish they could *really* have with the women who come here for jobs. They've played their part well, because the build-up to the sudden switch of tone has left me shocked by their brazen request, my heart suddenly racing at double the speed. Especially the 'highly fuckable' part. Not that it didn't create an instant bubble of lust deep in my stomach.

It's a good little role-play, I have to admit. I rise unsteadily, not really needing to act the wobbly part. "Of course," I say, making sure to look each one in the eye. "My panties may be a little wet, I do apologise in advance."

I can tell they're satisfied as they glance at each other with wicked grins. Before long I'm naked, apart from my heels, and the two men fuck me one after the other. For one I'm bent over the table, for the other I'm on my back, knees bent and legs wide. On the very same table where I'm quite sure they do proper interviews all the time.

Wow, it's quite a clever thing they've done there. I'm pretty sold on it, I must say. As far as I can see it's a bit of harmless fantasy for these men. What's the point in pretending guys like them don't think such thoughts when they're interviewing a pretty young intern? None at all! Dressing things up in PC clothing won't change what's going on in their heads. Far better to have me to bring their dreams to life than to actually mess with someone's career for real.

When they're done they let me dress, and go back into formal mode. "Thank you, Emma," each of them says as he offers his hand. "I'm sure we'll be in touch."

And I have a feeling they definitely will be.

That night I have an evening assignment — if that's the right word — with Charles. Last one before my birthday, actually, and the last time he'll be cooking for me before I get to make him some sushi!

But before all that, I'm down at a specialist for some jewellery to be inserted in my most intimate place. My counter-offer of fifty thousand was readily accepted, so here I am, legs open, with a strange man doing things to my vagina.

For once, though, the man is not going to fuck me. This, like all of the cosmetic and medical appointments Lucy sets up for me, is top-level specialist treatment. It's a far cry from the dodgy street corner tattoo artist where I first got my ears pierced and sent my mother into apoplexy when I was thirteen.

In spite of the growing knot of worry in my stomach at our impending conversation, I smile to myself at the thought that she went so mad about that. It's really nothing to the latest thing her miscreant daughter has gotten up to.

Well, whatever happens, at least she won't have to know about the clit ring. The idea of having it freaks me out just a little. I have a strange paranoia about catching it on some furniture or something, and having an awful, bloody accident.

But as the man works I'm warming to the notion of this new accoutrement. He's in his late twenties and clearly works out: his arms are like those of a heavyweight boxer! I can see most of them thanks to his tight, short-sleeved white t-shirt, and he's got a couple of gleaming dermal implants peeping out from the inside of his wrists. I wonder if he did them himself.

After all, he's doing the most intricate work imaginable on me. I'm glad I can't see what tools he's using down there. Apparently they don't use anaesthetic for this, so I can feel every stab of sensation.

Oh my, you can do that again.

God almighty, this is a man who knows how to find a clit. I suppose he'd have to, wouldn't he? *Oh yes, there it is!* Whatever he's doing, it's a sharp surge of pleasure each time he does it. Painful pleasure, that is. If you told me he was slowly pushing something thin and sharp through the hood, I'd believe you. I have to bite my lip to stop myself from making embarrassing noises.

"Does it hurt?" he says, looking up from his work and catching my eye. There's a twinkle in his — boy does he have a firm jawline! — and I think he knows he's asking me an awkward question.

"Not exactly," I snap grumpily as I try in vain to relax my tight grip on the edge of the examination table. And it hits me that the pain would be a good excuse for my sharp intakes of breath. "I mean, yes, it does."

I make an effort to turn my next moan into an 'ouch'. It does hurt, after all. Just in a very pleasant way.

He chuckles, knowing exactly what he's doing to me, and goes back to his project between my legs. Then the pinches turn to some kind of buzzing, and it's like he's using a tiny vibrator with a drill attached. But it's far tinier than anything you could buy in a sex shop. It's hitting a spot so small and so perfect that it's all I can do not to wriggle.

Christ, I'm not going to squirt in his face, am I? The awful prospect crosses my mind. I've just recently discovered that I'm capable of it. Fortunately it went down very well with the client on that particular night.

I manage to hold on, but only just. It's all over in ten minutes, but I'm breathing heavily and sticky with perspiration by the time he's done. Truth be told, I want the man to go down on me right now, or I might just explode. My legs are trembling and my control is on the brink.

Save it for tonight, I say to myself, thinking of Charles and hoping he's going to like what he finds. I assume Lucy is going to tell all clients of the new developments in my nether regions, but I'm quite sure Charles will approve. He worships pretty much anything I do.

Far too much the professional for my liking, my specialist leaves me to get dressed, assuring me that the ring can be taken out without too much trouble. Before he goes, he hands me a small mirror so that I can admire what he's done.

Just like when Miss Jackson left those pictures of my pussy, it's a surreal experience to look at what's going on down there. It's the biggest thing to happen to that part of my body in a long, long time. I'm still not sold, but it certainly does look pretty. It's a little larger and thicker than what I expected, almost like a small keyring.

I wonder, with a tiny fear gnawing at me, what Spurring has in mind with this little enhancement. He's only got three weeks to enjoy it, in keeping with the Christmas removal plan.

In the meantime, I get the fright of my life when I take my first few steps with the ring embedded right in my tender hood. Every pace is a like a little orgasm as it jiggles between my legs like a tiny, expert finger.

Oh my, it's going to be a long three weeks.

XX

At least once every day, I find myself standing at my huge window, staring out at frosty London and wondering when this dream will end. From the moment I snapped at my boss back in the summer, I've felt a little bit like all of this has been happening to somebody else. Some girl who had no idea what she was doing, but somehow landed up as the hottest property on the London escort scene.

Usually I just shake my head and smile to myself, still reeling at where I am and what I've become. Is this larger-than-life penthouse really mine? Am I the same woman who sat in an office chair for all that time, acting the dutiful employee and deluding myself that carefully crafted presentations would really be my ticket to a future? Fuck, how did we women get dragged into that when we have much more fun ways of making money? Maybe we've all been blinded by Pankhurst and her damned suffragettes.

Am I the same woman who whimpered when she thought she'd lost Rupert? The same woman who was so ashamed of training to be a prostitute that she couldn't even bear to say the word out loud? That was mere weeks ago! Now, in my mind, I'm proud. Like any successful businessperson, I suppose, I'm thrilled that I have clients who value my work so highly. And to be doing so well for myself. When Martin first mentioned this idea to me, and I almost slapped him for the suggestion, I'd have bet a million bucks that my journey wouldn't bring me here.

No, I'm *not* the same woman. I've changed so much that there's no other way to put it. At last, I've learned how to let myself enjoy myself. I've allowed Emma Carling to be what she really is. She's not some uptight, do-the-right-thing English rose any more. Before, she was hiding — though she didn't even know it.

Now, the real Emma Carling has come out, stood up and stripped off. The thrilling sex and the bountiful money are wonderful, of course. And they help validate the worth of what's happened to me. But to me, the greatest victory is feeling liberated and alive. Money really can't buy that.

I am still terrified of meeting up with my mother, of course. No amount of inner strength and self-love could quite prepare a girl for the news I'm planning on breaking. But I feel like I've got the chutzpah to see it through, at last. I need to do it. Along with the business of Spurring, keeping this secret is a niggle I want to get off my mind. Somehow.

In one of our frequent deep chats — usually when Alyssia is off somewhere — Sarah has made me realise that if I tell my parents, I can tell anyone. Cross that bridge first, and the rest will seem easy. If anything will teach me to be as *publicly* proud as I am inside myself, then telling my mother will do it. It's important that she knows, sure. But I have to remember that I don't need her approval.

Sarah, meanwhile, is having an exciting time. The moment her profile went online, her phone started buzzing like mad. There's business aplenty out there if she wants it.

"Who needs an agent, eh?" she teases me. "Look how many men want to pay me £150 an hour!"

There's a long list of gents who've applied for a slot in Sarah's completely open diary. Very few have pictures, of course, although quite a lot of them have been rated by other prostitutes who've serviced them. I can't quite get my head around all this — it's so much like eBay for sex!

I'm happy that I've got my agent, who vets all my clients and works in a world where the stakes are infinitely higher. I am glad I don't have to take my chances with any guy walking in off the street. That kind of thing is for Petra. Not that I say any of that to Sarah. She's doing the right thing for her situation and I want it to work out for her.

And unlike Petra, I think she can progress to better things.

"It's good money for an hour's work," I smile, trying not to come across as sarcastic. And I'm certainly not trying to be: it really is a good amount of money for sixty minutes of any kind of job! The fact that I'm getting obscenely spoilt right now doesn't change that.

But Sarah still comes and goes like the tides. Her enthusiasm seeps away from her after she finally books in a first client. She turns pale, and turns to me.

"Em, I don't know if I can really go through with it!" she says, showing me those eyes that look like they're about to sob. "I'm not as pretty as you; I didn't get such good grades; I'm not—"

For once, it's my turn to interrupt her and set her straight. "Hey, enough of that! You are as pretty as anyone, and who cares what that stupid school thinks? You are the one who helped me break through with that double-team thing we did, remember? Without your confident lead I might never have made it through that session. I might have gone running up the driveway and off into the hills, never to be seen again."

She smiles at this. And I kiss her. I do it so deeply that she knows, without a morsel of doubt, just how lovely and beautiful I think she is. Then I hold her hands and look into her eyes once again.

"This is only the beginning for you. When you've got some experience and all the five-star reviews I know you're going to get, I'm going back to Lucy and I'm going to get you on my team. Because I really, really want to play with you while I'm working. The thought of you and me entertaining a customer together makes me wetter than anything."

"I want that too, gorgeous!" she says, brightening in an instant.

"Okay then, go and enjoy some cock," I say. "You've not been with a man in a while: I think you need this!"

She laughs. "True. I've almost forgotten what it's like, thanks to you! Hey, but…why don't you join me and help me through my first client?"

I thought this suggestion might be coming, and I'm prepared for it. I shake my head. "Might be tempting, sure, but I'm not allowed. I'm exclusive with Lucy, you know? I think she'd go nuts if she thought I was available on the app for…" I must choose my words carefully, "A lower price."

She nods and sighs. "Well, nothing to worry about, I guess. It's sex with a man. And I get paid!"

"It really *is* as good as it sounds," I assure her. "Let's hope he's gorgeous too!"

After that I dress her in one of the many expensive gowns I've been given (my walk-in wardrobe is already beginning to creak), a pretty yellow number that's bright and perfect for a lunchtime appointment. I doubt it will stay on her for long, anyway.

We inspect the spare room, which has morphed into a minimalist sex den that I've finally been allowed to look at. Sarah and Alyssia have installed a double bed with a strong (and, I hope, discreetly quiet) base. They've made it attractive with deep red pillows and sheets, along with a thin white duvet. There's a cabinet by the bed with a candle on top, and a drawer stuffed full of condoms. Simple. And that's all that's needed for this chamber's animal purpose.

Then I give her a peck and leave her to it. I don't think she needs me hovering in the other room while this happens, even if she thinks she does. So I head to the café downstairs to peruse my book and drink a coffee, and text Alyssia (out gallivanting somewhere) not to go barging into the flat any time soon.

I can hardly keep my mind on the story, though. I keep thinking of Sarah's debut, and praying it goes well for her. I know that one good session will change her belief in herself, and my stomach is almost hurting from the anticipation of hearing her news in an hour or so.

And the image of her sucking a complete stranger off in my flat won't leave my head. It makes me far too wet to actually get any of my book read.

It's a huge relief to see Sarah's eyes shining when she opens the door for me. She's now dressed in her house gear: a t-shirt and grey tracksuit pants. Even though it's winter, you don't need any more than that in my well-insulated apartment. Not with all that sunlight that streams through the windows.

"Yes?" is all I ask, pulling her close as I walk into the hallway.

She sucks in a breath and gives me a look, all exaggerated and drunken-eyed. Another one of her tricks from drama school no doubt.

"Fuck me, yes!" she whispers.

I squeal and she squeals and we both jump up and down on the spot.

"So you did it! You've done it! You're like me! One of us!"

"God, Emma, why did I wait so long? We are the luckiest girls in London. Are we going to wake up any time soon?"

I've been asking myself that question ever since the summer, and I certainly don't know how to answer it from Sarah. I'm wary of her extreme mood swings, and I'm really not keen to risk bursting her bubble. At the same time, I'm scared of raising her expectations.

"Come on through to the lounge, I want to hear everything!" I say, taking her by the hand. "Is the money in?"

She shows me her phone, which displays the balance screen for the app. There's a healthy number on there. A one, followed by five and a zero. "Pre-paid," she giggles. "What have I been doing all my life?"

We sit down on the sofa and she regales me with the story of her first client, a well-groomed Danish man in his forties. Blonde and confident, he was visiting one of the major firms just around the corner. He had a three-hour break between meetings, and, at a loose end, he decided to indulge himself with my Sarah.

I'm so proud of her. And she's still popping with excitement.

"It didn't feel any different, Emma! It was like…it was just good, fun, sex. I opened the door and I wanted him straight away."

"So it was all completely natural then?"

She nods. "I was so nervous! But as soon as I saw him on the video screen, my heart just went crazy with excitement. I let him in, introduced myself and gave him a kiss on the cheek. Then I took his coat."

"Ooh, civilised!" I joke.

She hardly hears me, doesn't miss a beat. "After that I showed him into the room and, well, had some fun! I wanted to kiss him, so I did. And it all just happened. I forgot I was being paid or anything, except if he asked me to do this or that.

"But Em," she said, eyes shining bright and breath short and gaspy. "If a guy like that had told me to get down on my knees and, you know…I would have done it for nothing any day of the week! You should have seen his body! I think he's been working out on his other lunch breaks."

"It sounds like the perfect first experience, Sarah! I hope every guy is going to be as hot as he was."

I'm trying to gently bring her to earth and remind her it might not be this way every single time. Although kink probably won't be so much a part of her world just yet, as her clients are a little more time and budget-conscious. In short, they want a quick and easy fuck.

"Did you…get there?" I ask, curious.

"Twice! Did I mention how big he was? Once that monster

slipped into me, I was almost gone then and there. I can't believe I was nervous before. I mean, it's just sex!"

I nod, smile, and say nothing. The sun's beaming in through the glass and straight onto Sarah and me. It's warming my back and she's having to squint just to see me. It's another weekday that I could have been slaving over a laptop; and here I am sapping up the rays while comparing paid sex notes with my best friend and lesbian lover.

"You were so right, Emma," Sarah goes on. "I did need some cock! I've missed it."

A twang of something I don't quite like runs through my torso. And maybe she senses it: "Not that I would trade you for any man in the world, hear me? I wish you could have been there to share that cock with me."

And all at once I feel better. Not that I could really complain: she's never muttered a word about all the people I've been fucking since she moved here, despite the strong feelings we have for each other. I nod and put my hand on her thigh.

"We can make this work," I burst out, smiling now that I feel bright again. And I know she knows exactly what I mean.

Sarah gradually starts seeing more men, but — thank God! — she remains as ravenous for me as ever. And now that she has money, she's beginning to give me little treats. I find flowers on the bed, she takes me up the London Eye — shockingly, I'd never been —and insists we plan ourselves a little getaway on her.

And best of all, to celebrate her first client, she orders champagne once again, insisting on Scott as our delivery man.

This time she's planned it so that it's his last job of the day, and she doesn't breathe a word about the delivery. She just lights some scented candles and puts me in the bath. When I whine that she's not with me, she scurries off on the pretext of getting us a drink. She comes back with a drink all right — plus a naked Scott.

We devour him again, both in and out of the water. He's a lucky boy, he is. And I think I love Sarah.

Alyssia is still around, but not spending a whole lot of time in my apartment. It's not like we've fallen out; I think she's just being sensitive. In fact, she tells me so. She doesn't want to take advantage of my flat, and I think she knows that Sarah and I need our own space. Which is not to say she doesn't share our bed and play with us when the mood takes us all. Like Sarah, I've given her a key, and she has my total trust.

She's been given a little three-month trial with her agency, and it's going extremely well. It doesn't sound quite at Lucy's level, and for now it's not an exclusive thing for her, but the earnings are still a cut above what the app would bring her. Though I've told her she's welcome to use our 'sex room' if she wants to try that option post-trial, she says she'd rather use her own place for that. And now that she's got her big break, she's decided to stay in London for a while: at least until she helps us settle my score with Spurring. So Alyssia is on the lookout for a digs of her own.

I tell her she's welcome at mine, but we both know that it's more kind than I need to be, much as I love her. My bond with Sarah is getting stronger by the day, and my home has to be our sanctuary up to a point. I quickly realise that I don't think I really want Sarah working regularly from my flat.

Even if she starts paying rent, it's not about the money. It's about us having a refuge. And avoiding any awkward moments. After all, as far removed as I now am from the shy little English girl I barely recognise from my past, things are easier if I can come home safe in the knowledge there won't be a strange man getting dressed in the hallway. Not only that, but I would get tired if I had to keep on making myself scarce while she did her work.

Not that she's asked me to, of course, but I think I prefer it that way. I've been caught out once or twice already, finding myself stuck in our room whilst she entertained a man. I could hear her groans and his grunts, and the little seed of envy took root in me when that happened. I didn't much like it.

Also, she made the mistake of showing one of her clients the bathroom, and she had to work hard to talk him away from fucking her whilst looking over London.

I'm not ashamed to admit that I don't want to share my dream bathroom with anybody but Sarah and our own guests. So we agree that it's best we find her another 'office' for her work, if she's going to carry on with this.

And since I don't think wild horses could drag the ever-beaming Sarah away from prostituting herself now, we agree to start looking for a little place where she can entertain clients. Who are all leaving her five-star reviews, of course. How could they not?

Things are looking up for us all. Both Sarah and Alyssia have made big strides, and I'm thrilled for them. We've got some more exciting house-hunting to come, and everyone's loving life. The Australian — and Latifa, texting like mad from Newcastle — won't let us forget the plan to catch Spurring.

There's something exciting about our little conspiracy...I *think*. Although I'm starting to wonder if it really *is* Spurring. Have I leapt to conclusions? My heart beats a little quicker — for more than one reason — every time I think about the appointment I have with 'him' in two nights' time. The clit ring is a constant, tingling reminder of that.

Before this, though, I have one appointment that fills me with dread. And it's not a client. It's my mother.

XXI

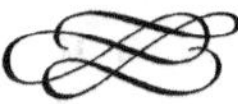

J don't know what makes me more nervous; the gravity of
what I'm about to say to my mum or the thought of the
noises Sarah was making with her client only an hour ago.

The thought of my mother hearing either of these makes my
head pound with worry. Or that she might look in the sex room,
which is slightly too pornographic not to raise a comment of some
sort. I'm going to have to tell her it's a cupboard.

I'm acutely aware that I'm making my mother's coffee with an
outrageous espresso machine that, as far as she is concerned, I
couldn't possibly afford. My mind is latching onto stupid little
things like this, as if this whole damn palace of mine isn't already
one massive giveaway that something big has changed in my life.

Why didn't I meet her 'off-site' again? Oh yes, so that I wouldn't
chicken out of saying what I need to say. Christ, but that's *so*
tempting right now. All that confidence and belief and pride in what
I do has fallen off the edge of the eleventh floor; right off the
balcony I can see behind my mother's questioning but innocent eyes.

I'm just about running out of small talk and coffee to fiddle with
when Sarah appears, fresh from the shower. I swear I go red at the

mere thought of the reason she's having to clean herself. It's barely half an hour since she ushered her client out of the flat and I gave the whole place a furious spray, paranoid that it smelt of sex. The timing was all a little too close for comfort.

I've asked Sarah to stay and at least say hello. I want the distraction, though I don't want her to hang around and make me feel self-conscious. I know my mum will like her, because it's impossible not to like the warm yet vulnerable Sarah. She's a hug magnet like I've never known.

"Hi Mrs Carling!" beams Sarah, skipping the introductions and bounding over for a handshake.

"This is my friend Sarah, Mum. Well, my room-mate too."

Sarah gives me a naughty wink when she's sure my mother isn't looking, and I wince. *Please don't let's get into lesbian love right now!* She's just messing with me, of course. She's been fully briefed that the prostitution thing will be more than enough of a shock for one day. I'm already half-tempted to have an ambulance on standby, in case Mum has a heart attack when she hears the news.

"Good to meet you, Sarah. So, are you the one with the rich father paying for this place?"

It's an attempt at a joke from my mother, but it says everything about her preconceptions of the world. The patriarchal world that's all she's ever known, where a woman selling her body could only mean shame and poverty, not status and wealth. Where a woman couldn't possibly have a place like this on her own money, unless she were the queen. I suspect my mother hasn't always been entirely comfortable with the idea of me having any kind of job at all. Her visions of the future, I know, are filled with grandkids.

My mother's throwaway remark plants a little seed in my brain too.

"I'll let Emma answer that, Mrs Carling. Don't forget to give her the full tour now, will you Emma? Just leave my room out of it — the place is an absolute tip."

Her room? But we sleep together! She jerks her head towards the sex room, and suddenly I get it. She's engineered a good reason for me not to open *that* door, and at the same time made sure I don't have to answer the 'where does Sarah sleep' question. Good girl! I'm so glad my friends think ahead more than I do.

"I won't!" I grin, hopefully looking less nervous than I really am.

"I have to pop out now," announces Sarah, right on cue. "Pleasure to meet you, Mrs Carling."

"Likewise," replies my mother, looking a little baffled by her brief encounter with Sarah.

When Sarah's gone, I stall things a little longer by taking my mother on a tour of the house while her coffee cools. Inevitably, she has no idea what to make of it. The poor woman has simply never seen anything like it. She's born and bred on suburban London terraces.

She is quite literally speechless as I show her around, suddenly remembering I haven't warned Alyssia not to come bursting in and shouting about what she just did with a client. Oh God. *Let's hurry this along.*

The bathroom clearly makes her head spin. She's not at all sure how that glass-sided bath tub can possibly be possible. "Is this…safe, Emma? How strong is that glass?"

I chuckle. "Oh, Mum, I think these builders know what they're doing! It's probably the same stuff those see-through floors on office mezzanines are made of."

She doesn't look convinced at all. "Can people see in, then?"

I shrug, and then go red as I realise I haven't really even thought about that. Shameless, I know.

"Well, I don't know, but they'd have to have a space telescope, wouldn't they!"

"I suppose," she murmurs, slowly taking in the fact that there's nothing but a wide stretch of river between my window and some far lower buildings on the far bank of the Thames.

"Come on, let's go and sit down," I announce, feeling uncomfortable at the thought of the things I've done in this room with Sarah. And Scott. And Alyssia. And Latifa. This is no place for my mother.

"Sure," she says. "I'm really very curious to know what's been happening in your life."

"I thought you might be," I say with a big gulp as I hand her my home-brewed latte and we sit down on the sofa. "Well, I have found a job."

She raises her eyebrows. "Yes? What is it?"

God, I really want to tell her Sarah has a rich father and I'm just lucky enough to be bunking here while I'm working as a receptionist somewhere.

And it's not too late to say that. She's met my friend and she would probably buy it. I can just say Sarah is a school friend (true, kind of) that I've reconnected with and she's got a high-flying job and she's happy for me to stay here and just pay the bills.

Fuck, am I really going to lie after all this time spent thinking about how this day would go? It's the one scenario I never played out. Not once.

My mother is still looking at me, waiting for me to come up with something. It's a look I remember from when I was very young, and she would ask me if I had taken sweets out of the jar. Although this time, I'm quite sure she doesn't know the answer already. The truth about me can't possibly have crossed her mind.

She didn't raise me to be puritanical or a good girl or never to think of sex outside of marriage. All of the above was merely implied, because she never spoke about sex at all. Neither of my parents did. Which is exactly what's making this so difficult. That fucking English 'education' that was no education at all. We never even had a birds and bees chat, and now the topic for our first conversation about sex is that her daughter has become a highly paid tart.

Shit, but I'd better say something.

I'm so bad at lying. I just can't say all of this is Sarah's.

"Okay, Mum, I've learned a new trade. I'm, er, a— "

And of course, I can't say it.

I find myself changing tack, no longer in any control of what comes out of my mouth.

"I'm a masseuse," is what emerges. The best euphemism for a whore that I can think of.

"A what?" she says, looking blank.

Christ, she's making this even more difficult than it needs to be. Of course, she didn't grow up in a world where any kind of massage was heard of.

"Er, it means you give massages, you know?"

There's a silence. I am suddenly praying she doesn't understand the connotations that entails for some women. Because it's not strictly a lie, what I've just said. Some of my work has included an element of massage. Particularly on certain body parts.

"Oh, I think I know what you mean. Like sports people get?"

She really isn't getting the connotations at all.

"A bit like that," I say. "Mine are just more about relaxation and enjoyment. It's very popular nowadays and it's only a short course to learn the basics. I didn't want to tell anyone while I was learning, in case I gave up and didn't like it. But I quite like the work and I quickly found an agency looking to take people on. The skill is quite in demand."

I'm not sure how much sense I'm making, but I'm pretty sure I'm not technically telling any lies. I'm just shaving some of the uglier realities out of the story. One thing's for sure: if I'm going to make her understand, I'm going to have to come right out and say it straight.

Not sure I can now. I'm physically incapable of moving my lips to say the words.

Come on Emma, you're physically capable of so much more than you ever thought. You've proven that already this year.

"It is…for women, then?" asks my mother, and I can't detect if it's hope or innocence in her voice. For the first time I'm beginning to wonder if she's as naïve as I've always thought she is.

"Yes, quite often," I reply truthfully. "But also for men." I pause. "Some of the rich ones in this area have quite stressful lives, and the money's pretty good."

"As good as all this?" she asks, thankfully steering away from any further questions about the work itself.

"Well, Sarah is also working, you know...she's got a big job nearby and she does really well for herself. I definitely owe her plenty."

Again, not exactly lies.

I can tell she's got a lot of questions, but isn't sure how to ask them.

"You did a course, you say?"

"Short but intense, I guess," I say truthfully. "I've come to realise that most of what they teach in university can be covered in a couple of weeks. It's better to learn on the job."

"So you have a qualification from this course?"

"A little diploma, yes," I say, before hurriedly adding, "I don't think I'll be getting anything in the mail. These things only exist on the internet these days."

"I see," she says, looking a lot like she doesn't. "So this agent makes appointments for you?"

"That's it. They've got a little studio and I just go along for a few hours a day. The times are quite variable."

The studio thing is the first outright lie I've told. I feel terrible.

I smile, thinking of a way to make myself feel better, as well as avoiding more questions: "I can give you a massage next time I come round, Mum! Then you'll understand what it's all about."

"Well, yes, I'd like to know," she says. "I don't think I can even picture it."

"Fine!" I say in a hurry. "Next week then. I'll show you! You'll feel great!"

I'm hoping that if I can introduce her to the concept via something resembling a clothed Thai massage, it might stop her asking questions about the technicalities of how I do it with my clients. Ideally for the rest of time.

I have a vague feeling I'm digging a big hole of lies for myself here. In fact, I know I am. But it succeeds in changing her tack for now.

"But how much does this place cost, Emma! Nobody could earn that much, could they? What are they paying you?"

This is still difficult. "Of course they can — this whole building is full of renters, isn't it? Sarah's doing really well, and I get a lot of tips. The agency charges quite a lot. They only look for really wealthy customers, and people around here have far more money than sense, you know?"

I'm not sure she does. She's looking a little glassy-eyed. What's she making of it all? There are so many obvious questions for her to ask. *Wealthy, eh? So what are they expecting? Are the men naked? Do they grope you? Do you have to do happy endings?*

But these are the questions *my* generation would ask, not hers. Even if they were on the tip of her tongue — and I can't quite work out if her mind has even gone that far — I'm not sure she'd actually put them into words. They would, after all, be terribly rude things to ask about.

I could put this beyond all doubt right now. "Mum, I am a prostitute. I have sex with very wealthy men for money. There's a £50,000 ring in my clit as we speak. And that's what's paying for all of this."

But I don't say that. I just can't bring myself to do it. I can leave this hanging and it can nag away at me all the way to Christmas. The thought of doing that almost brings a tear to my eye. But the thought of speaking the full truth is like ice in my veins. I can delay this a little longer, do it all in baby steps. Maybe wait till she actually asks me outright, if she ever does. Saying 'yes' will be easier than actually spelling it out.

What a chicken I'm being.

Come on, spit it out, Emma Carling!

"So how's dad?" I ask.

Lame. I barely hear her answer me. I'm so mad I'm going to let her leave here without the full truth. I'm so cross that I'm putting it off. And I know the moment is gone.

XXII

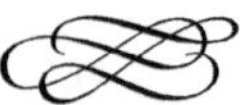

I don't think I've ever changed so much between birthdays. Last year was filled with tears and angst about getting older, being single and drowning in a relentless, choppy, violent sea of work. I seem to recall a particularly enraging conference call that day. One which left me grumpy throughout evening drinks with a few of my close friends.

This year I am somebody completely different. A happier, healthier and barely recognisable Emma. And my first day of being twenty-seven gets off to a spectacular start as Sarah wakes me up with the gentlest of licks to my clit. For a moment I think I'm dreaming. Then, groggy with sleep, I realise what's happening and succumb to the most delicious, lazy and effortless orgasm.

"Happy birthday Emma," she murmurs as she crawls up the bed and plants a soft, loving kiss on my lips.

The sun is pouring into the room and I drift off again as Sarah disappears to make coffee and order croissants from the posh bakery downstairs. I'm content as a kitten, happy that I've got a clear diary until my appointment with Charles tonight. Sarah re-appears with a tray, complete with a single rose and a small, gift-wrapped box.

"Really?" I say as I sit upright and she settles in beside me. "The way you woke me up was more than enough of a present you know!"

"It's nothing really," she says. "But go on, open it!"

I wonder what it could be. I remove the lid with my fingers, and find a shiny black chess piece resting on a velvet cushion inside. It's a knight, but not just any knight. It's a finely crafted item that is as much ornament as it is plaything. I pull it out with an excited smile. On closer examination, it's thick glass filled with what looks like ink, which comes to life with a subtle swirl as you move it. It's very creative. The sort of thing you see in arty magazine shoots. And it's the perfect present, because it's too indulgent for me ever to buy myself.

"I love it — the dark knight! But are we going to play chess with just one piece?"

"No, silly! Let me get the rest…"

She eases off the bed and scrabbles about beneath it, carefully emerging with the rest of the set. I gasp as I see the board and all the pieces brought together. It's a truly amazing piece of art. The white pieces are filled with a bright liquid of their very own. It's the colour of milk, just as striking in its own way. Even more funkily, each square on the thick glass board is also filled with alternating black and white.

It's a living, breathing chess board. Perfect for my bare coffee table. And it's dawning on me why she went for it.

"I thought it might bring back some memories," she grins, recalling the game of human chess we played at school. "I know you didn't get to play as much as you wanted that day…"

I smile and shake my head. "You have a good memory, Sarah Smith! But you're right. I did get a little bit left out — thank you. I can't wait to play!"

I lean across to give her a huge hug.

"Woah, don't knock the tray over!" she scolds. "Why don't you pour us some coffee before you spill it all over the floor?"

I smile and do as she asks. When I lift the first of the upturned coffee mugs, I notice something unusual beneath it.

"Hmm," I murmur, picking up the small tube and suspecting that she's slipped another present onto my breakfast tray. "Chocolate body paint!"

"I couldn't resist a saucy little something to go with the chess," she explains. "We have unfinished business with paint too, remember?"

Ah yes! The time I was busy washing her black-smeared body down after the chess game, and couldn't go through with the whole lesbian thing. That feels like a lifetime ago. What a clever, thoughtful gift idea!

"I see what you're getting at," I say, breaking into a smile. "Good thinking! I reckon I'll be able to finish the job this time."

"Not till you've had your fair share of chocolate though," she winks.

I love the presents she's chosen. She hasn't gone for the easy or the obvious. Rather, she's chosen something that has meaning for both of us and our relationship. I wish I could pick gifts as smartly as she's done.

We munch happily through breakfast, then take a long and lazy bath before meeting Alyssia for lunch. I meet a couple of my best school friends for coffee in the afternoon, feeling so good about myself that I come very close to breaking down and telling them exactly what it is that's giving me the glow they keep picking up on.

There's a phone call from my parents too, all the more awkward because there's no mention of anything I discussed with my mother at the apartment. It's just the usual birthday wishes, but they do both sound a little distant. I presume mum has spoken with dad, and neither of them knows quite what to say. I hope it will pass, one way or another.

I feel momentarily heartbroken when mum says, "I love you,"

before ringing off. The feeling that I've let her down terribly brings tears to my eyes, but it's not long before the sentiment passes. I've gotten so much better at reminding myself that I'm not a criminal or a bad person. It's safe to say I don't have the backing of my family, but they're from a different generation and I'm a grown woman.

I spend some time on the sofa replying to messages and flicking through my Facebook wall. Miss Jackson and Martin both call to give me their best wishes, but the most exciting message from the day is from Charles.

Happy birthday, gorgeous one. I'm looking forward to your birthday dinner. Yum. Licking my lips...Charles

Rippling with anticipation, I start thinking of the evening around four o'clock. Technically, this is a work assignment, but I've pretty much forgotten that I get paid for my time with Charles. I adore my hours with him and adore the way he makes me feel. Plus, it was his generous offer to take care of my schooling that got me into this game. I want to please him so much tonight, after all he's done for me.

I hop on a tube and gather ingredients from a special dealer in Soho. Rice, seaweed wrap, avocado, tuna, salmon...I'm not going for anything too extravagant. I almost forget to pick up some wasabi that looks like one of my high school science experiments, and the same pickled ginger that had me mildly addicted during my classes.

Then I come home and decide what to wear. Sarah helps me, full of excitement. I know it's coming off before dinner is served, but I still want to wow him when I show up at the door. Even though, deep down, I know I could arrive in rags and still turn him on.

I settle on a white blouse and a short, black skirt. It's my favourite combination these days, and I often opt for it if there aren't specific dress instructions. Maybe because it's a little bit like the work gear from the life I've left behind, albeit with a far shorter hemline.

Since it's my birthday, I give the panties a miss.

I do wear a pink bra, though, just so its hem can peep out above my top button and excite him. I don black heels and pop my hair into a tight ponytail. I'm good to go.

Half an hour and an interminable taxi ride later, Charles welcomes me with his usual sweet kiss, and gently places a glass of white wine into my hand before shutting the door behind me. Even though I'm here to make him dinner, he's already making me feel like a princess.

"I've barely done any work today, you know," he smiles as he sits me down on the sofa for a moment. "I think I should have booked you last night, so I could wake up next to you on your birthday."

My heart melts. "You should have," I whisper.

"Well, I had to pick up your present today," he admits. "It took me so long to decide that I left it until absolutely had to pick one out."

"Ooh, pick what out?" I ask, swimming in curiosity.

He fishes in his pocket and produces a black case, clearly one that houses a ring. *Surely not?*

"I rather hope you'll wear this, Emma," he says, sounding unusually uncertain. "If I ever looked for a wife, she'd be you…"

For the second time in the day, my eyes cloud up. I look at him, not sure what I'm feeling besides a lot of emotion. I wouldn't really have said yes, would I? I thought I knew the answer to that, but now I'm not so sure.

I try to gather myself with a nod and a smile, wondering if I really wanted this to be the real thing. If I wanted to be the one woman who changed his mind about monogamy. Things that seemed so simple earlier are less so now.

I open the box and I'm greeted by a bright diamond nestled on a ring of gold. It's the most beautiful jewel I've ever seen, yet it's a long way from ostentatious.

"Of course I'll wear this for you," is all I can muster for the moment. "It would be my honour."

He takes hold of the box again and removes the ring before slipping it over the third finger on my left hand. It's a snug fit.

"Happy birthday, Emma," he says with his warm smile. "Now come and show me your sushi skills."

It takes me a while to calm down and focus on anything apart from his gift, which keeps catching my eye. But I get my head straight by the time I've unpacked the shopping and told him all about my day. Including the rude awakening and funny presents from this morning. He loves to hear everything about me and Sarah.

It's funny to see him leaning against the kitchen counter, watching me, instead of taking care of everything. He points me in the direction of a suitable knife and cutting board, then watches me quietly while I prepare our feast. Or his feast, rather. I'm not sure how I'm supposed to get any if I'm to be the table.

I'm not nervous about the preparation. Charles makes me feel far too comfortable. And besides, I've been well-trained. It goes better than I could hope, and the creations I'm assembling on his set of long, sparkling, white plates looks reasonably smart. It's actually making me salivate just a little.

It's slow going, but as usual we've got plenty to talk about, against the backdrop of some light jazz. It fills the room from every direction: Charles must have had the finest acoustics engineers in London build his sound system. I believe it was a shared love of music that first brought him together with my friend Martin. Thank God it did!

After almost an hour and a half of careful chopping, squeezing and wrapping – I definitely don't have the speed to do this in a sushi bar – I pour out the last of the soy sauce into a little dish and add it to a small plate with the ginger and the wasabi. I've managed twenty-four pieces of sushi, and I'm pretty satisfied.

Now my heart begins to thud.

I turn to Charles. "Well, voilà," I declare. "Your sushi, Sir."

"All I need is my beautiful table, then," he says, striding to a drawer and pulling out some gleaming metal chopsticks. Lucky he's sophisticated enough to have that sort of thing in the kitchen. I forgot to think of it, of course.

I nod, trying for some reason to prevent a wicked grin spreading across my face. "Where would you like to dine, Sir?"

He gestures towards the casual dining table in the centre of his kitchen, and picks up the remote that controls the lights. He switches off the lamps directly above the table, but turns on all those around the perimeter. Amazingly, he can swivel them by remote. And they all turn to face the table, creating a dim theatre with spotlights on the stage.

"Maybe if you leave the room I can get set up perfectly for you?"

He smiles and nods his approval. "Okay. Call when you're ready."

After he leaves I quickly shed my blouse and my skirt. I'm used to undressing every day, but this is different and particularly exciting. I'm glad I didn't wear panties, because they'd be a sodden mess already. I snap off the pink bra, which leaves me in only the heels. I think he'll like me keeping those on.

Naked, I grab the plates and arrange them carefully on the table. I crawl between them and lie on my back, wincing a little at the cool feel of the wood.

Piece by piece, I take the sushi and arrange it along my body as artfully as I can. I sit up and start with my legs, rolling them open and outwards for a bit more surface area. My pussy responds to that move the way it always does. But I have to be careful not to shudder or move, or everything will fall off.

It gets trickier as I lie down again and have to work at an awkward angle, craning my neck. But it's easy to balance the food on my stomach and torso. I try to perch some on my nipples, but I don't think it's going to work. I settle for putting the pieces above, below and between my breasts. And leave a couple of teasers well south of my belly button and at the top of my thighs.

I test that I can breathe in and out without anything falling, then carefully croak to Charles that he can come back.

I close my eyes, focusing only on keeping still. But I can hear his footsteps loud and clear as they come close, then pause.

"Oh my," he says. "That is my idea of a feast! And I can see the most luscious dessert down there between your legs."

I don't speak, for fear of destabilising my creation. He needs to get cracking.

He reads my thoughts, of course, and makes a start with the chopsticks. I keep my breathing quiet and just smile at him as I watch him eat.

"Looks beautiful, and tastes even better, Emma. This is a real delight. Thank you."

"Thank *you*," I whisper while breathing in. Nowhere is safe yet, as he's picking morsels at random from all over me. Every now and then he feeds me one. It's definitely my best sushi effort yet, and I'm one happy girl right now. Although it's torture trying to keep still when he impishly pinches my nipples with the chopsticks. I frown my displeasure, and he chuckles.

"I'm nearly done here," he grins. "With the sushi at least."

I cast my eyes down my body. It's true: he's demolished nearly every piece. I'm thrilled. He must really have liked it to have devoured the lot like that.

I'm acutely aware that he's left the pieces around my centre till last. He abandons the chopsticks now, and begins to nip them directly off my body. As he takes the last piece from the top of my thigh, I can feel his breath on my wide open sex. I whimper at the rushing heat.

"And now for that final course," he announces with glee, as he swallows. I open my eyes, thrilled that the whole sushi thing got full marks, and watch him make his way around to the foot of the table, his face reappearing between my knees.

He reaches forward and slides me gently towards him, pulling me by the hips. I bend my knees without being asked, and he takes a seat.

Bizarre. But hot.

He leans in and does what he does so well. I'm writhing and squirming within seconds, and that's before he even reaches my clit. Right now all he's doing is tasting my pussy with long, languid tongue strokes. He's enjoying his dessert like it really is an ice cream.

His hands hold my hips steady as I begin to buck. His tongue is enough, especially as it slides onto my clit and begins to flick like that of a searching serpent. I gasp and groan as he keeps dining out on me, my head tossing this way and that under the bright rays of the spotlights.

My second orgasm of the day is a big and violent one, totally different from this morning's sleepy and beautiful wake-up shudder. I couldn't have planned it any better. Yet there's still something missing.

"You won't stop there, will you?" I ask, worried. "I need you inside me Charles."

"You've got it, birthday girl," he says. "But I've had enough of this kitchen. Let's go somewhere more comfortable."

I nod, and let him pick me up off the table in his strong arms, lying back exactly as I was when he ate me out. I feel light-headed with happiness as he carries me up the stairs and lays me gently down on his bed.

It's another four hours before we sleep, so endless and so passionate is our lovemaking. And that's exactly what it is with Charles. He doesn't do everything a man can do, but he does things to me that nobody else can.

I couldn't have asked for a more perfect birthday.

XXIII

The gentle pull between my legs has me wincing and writhing on the very threshold between pleasure and pain. Every sense and every thought is consumed by the feeling around that little ring.

It's tiny, yet that wispy slip of metal is the centre of my universe right now. Friends, family, worries, fear and plans have all slipped into a kind of grey light. Like pre-dawn. Which, beyond my blindfold and this room, cannot be far away now.

I've been kept in this position since midnight, totally at *his* mercy. My blindfold is tighter than before. And my treatment has gone to the next level.

My hands were bound by Esmeralda when I arrived back at the house whose name I do not know. As far as I can feel, it's a coarse, thick rope that holds my wrists together. Not behind my back, but on my lap. Very close to where I might be able to touch myself. But not close enough.

When she tied me she had already removed my clothing with neither sympathy nor ceremony. Only my panties and heels were left after her stripping. She pulled the clothes off me in the entrance hallway, then guided me into what I assume is the usual room. She pushed me into a seated position on what I feel to be a table or a desk, and made me hold out my wrists for binding.

I knew that desk would be wet before long.

The room is colder than ever; I can feel the tautness of my nipples without needing to look at them or touch them. Neither of which I can do right now.

And then she attached the clamps.

If sitting there bound, blindfolded and almost naked had my heat rising, it's what she did next that took me to an extraordinary place. Her fingers pushed my panties aside, and I gasped to feel them brush my lips as they sought out my new piece of jewellery. The tiny, almost innocent thing that this man paid a fortune for me to implant in a place that sends me to heaven.

I heard a click, then felt a tug. Another little gasp: she attached something to my clit ring. Christ, what was it? Another rope? A chain? She had me spread my legs so that now I can't even feel what's pulling on me.

"You will be punished if you move any part of your body from now on," she said, sounding noticeably harsher than on my previous visits. Keep your legs open and do not manipulate your hands. You will be restrained by your ring. Do not squirm, or you may be harmed. Do not orgasm."

Harmed? What exactly does she mean? Harmed by my own movements or by someone else? An unspeakably erotic shiver gripped me and ripped through my body as I whispered my acquiescence, and I felt the pulls tighten as she did something a couple of yards away in front of me.

Tighter again. *Oh my.* Another tug. Ouch, that could be too much! And that's just where the pull stopped. At the very moment I bite my lip to stop my yelp. Or, rather, that's where it stopped getting any tighter. The tension stayed on exactly that point. On the brink of too much. Which is also the edge of orgasm. Fuck.

I heard her walking away. She must have tied me to something. I couldn't begin to fathom what it was, or whether it might have been something mechanical, exerting an ever so tiny constant pull. I was forbidden from moving; it had me locked in a place where I might not last. Because I wanted to squirm already.

I could feel that if I did that — even a tiny twitch — my clit would be in danger of damage. I had to do as she had ordered, and keep still.

That was at least three hours ago. The cuckoo clock told me so, a regular reminder of how long I've been kept there, driven to distraction.

And not just by the nagging, edgy and dangerous insistence at my clitoris. Nor even the position, thrillingly submissive and rounded off by a ball gag shoved in my mouth. Nor just the sharp, tangy sensation of the nipple clamps. There's also the sense that *he* is here, watching me.

It's because she asked him if he was pleased, and then left the room. I didn't hear him reply. Either it's because he merely nodded. Or maybe it's a bluff on her part, and I'm alone. For the first little while, I don't know if it's just him, or a dozen men, or nobody. Not knowing how many people, if anyone, can see me displayed and suffering and shuddering like this, is the purest form of sexual torture anybody can ever have dreamed up.

I strain my ears for signs of life or movement. I swear I hear the pages of a book turn on occasion, but I wonder if it's my mind playing tricks. I want him to be watching me, but not as much as I want him to take me now. I need a release in more ways than one. Half an orgasm has been churning around me for half the night now, but I'm not allowed to come. And if I did, I know it would hurt me. The cord, or whatever it is, is too tight.

I cannot jeopardise my precious clit. I must deny it, and sit tight.

This is supposed to be the night the plan I cooked up with the girls really gets going. This is the night I show no fear, and instead win his confidence. It's the night I show how much more I want; how I start to earn his trust. It will be a slow process, but I need to show that I am too much in his thrall to ever betray him. That I want only to serve him, even if he shows his face.

Will I need to act? My thoughts on that keep going in circles. I'm rolling back and forth between ecstasy and danger, all the while feeling desperately uncomfortable. My bladder is filling and my muscles threaten to seize. I do not believe I could walk right now, trapped in this position for so long. My hands are numb, partly thanks to my tightly bound wrists and partly thanks to the cold.

I keep thinking about my pain score from the doctor, and how I can take just about anything. I draw strength from that, even as my jaw begins to thud with discomfort from the ball gag.

And yet none of the hurt does anything to extinguish the fire inside me.

When the clock strikes five, there's finally a move. Footsteps. Male footsteps, without a doubt. On the floorboards I've come to know well. I hope my time has come.

Now he's in front of me, breathing hotly and heavily on my forehead. I can smell his scent and I *know* it's him. One hand falls gently on my stomach, and another grips my hair like it's never been gripped, pulling it with savage intent so that my head rips back and my nose, grappling for air, points at the ceiling.

I have to tighten every muscle in my core to keep my pussy safe as he does this.

"We're going for a walk now. Come with me." A delicious double meaning, whispered as before, but louder and with more menace.

I nod and make a sound as best I can, feeling drool rolling down from the corner of my mouth as he gives my hair a final tug and lets go of it.

He moves away, and I feel the tug on my clit go slack. He must have unclipped it from whatever held it at the other end. Instinctively I take the chance to move some aching muscles, and he doesn't stop me.

"Stand up, slowly."

Very carefully I lower one heel to the floor and put some weight on it, little by little. It trembles, but, taking my time, I manage to stand up. I feel like a newborn lamb. The sensation of blood rushing to my extremities is almost as exquisite as an orgasm would be. It gets even better as he frees my wrists.

"You will need your hands to crawl on all fours," he says as I try to shake some life into them. "The nipple clamps and gag will remain. I don't want to hear any more of your shit."

That was nasty. No client has said that kind of thing, unprompted, unless we're clearly in role play. It's come from nowhere. And it feels real. I feel sure again that this is Spurring, and it's a timely reminder that I *do* want to get back at him.

Playing along as best I can, I nod and sink to the ground. On all fours.

Like a dog on a lead.

And that lead isn't around my neck. It's tied to my most erotic place and it's emerging right out of the top hem of my panties. As he pulls it tighter, bringing that familiar tug back into my world, I can feel leather crawling all the way up my torso, between my breasts and past my right cheek. This may quite literally be a dog lead.

The *fucker*.

But I'm wet. I just know I'm wet.

"Walk," he commands. And as he says it, I know I flood a little more.

He leads me and I crawl. Floorboards, carpet, floorboards. He opens a door, and closes it behind me. We're somewhere brighter, perhaps the entrance hallway. Who can see me? Only him? I can never know.

"We're going up the stairs now, so keep up or that metal and your pussy flesh are going to have a violent disagreement, you fucking bitch," he hisses.

His words make me want to tear off my blindfold and punch him in the nuts. But I'm a professional. He won't really hurt me. I'm being paid. I keep telling myself this. And yet I know it's personal with him, and I don't deserve the venom.

I hate him. I wanted to tear his throat out as he said those words. Yet the fire in my belly is hotter than anything I've ever felt as he pulls me up the carpeted stairs and I follow. His little bitch. Gagged, blindfolded and led by her clit ring.

I want this hotness to go away, but I can't make it. I must hate him; I must stick to the plan. So I must like him. I have never, ever been so confused or unsure of myself.

Nor so aroused.

We enter another room now, him still leading me by a leather leash attached to the polished jewel on my hood. I am every inch his slave as I hear him close the door behind us.

It's warmer in here. I think there is a fire going. He drags my aching body harder across the room now, and I must crawl fast to keep up with him. *How hard would he really pull me there?* More than anything, that's the question making my vagina blaze right now.

"I'm tying you up to the mantelpiece, Emma Carling," he says. "You're mine now. I own your clit and lead you where I want to."

Fuck. How long does *now* last? I know I'm booked until seven. I have never heard him say so much. He used my full name again. My brain is whirling as much as my pussy is. I don't know anything anymore.

It's no longer tight. I'm still in doggy position, but the leather hangs down loose below my breasts. I'm almost comfortable, and certainly begging for more. He makes me do exactly that, kneeling back on my heels and looking up at him.

"Open wide," he orders, before shoving a finger and a thumb into my cheeks and ripping out my ball gag. I pant with relief as my jaw is finally released and drool spills down my chin. I am glad it's gone, but some part of me wants my wrists tied again.

I want to be tied up by Spurring. *Jesus, Emma, will you get out of your own way? You have a plan!* I'm trying to focus, but once again my horniness threatens to cloud my thoughts. It has done already. The throbbing in my clit and the tremble in my body tells me that.

I'm supposed to make him get ready to reveal himself. He doesn't look like he's in the mood. And I can barely speak anyway; my tongue is like lead and my jaw hardly working. I'm consumed by my need for orgasm.

And now he unzips himself and enters my mouth. God, it's an attack. He mouth-fucks me like nothing I've ever experienced, ramming the back of my throat like an invading army's cannonballs. I grunt along with every one of his thrusts, unable to even pretend any more. My eyes are closed and I'm on the verge of coming just as I feel him tighten.

I'm fully expecting a release into my mouth that will take me over the edge, but somehow he holds his twitching member in check, and grabs a fist of my hair again.

This makes the last pull feel like something that would have happened in the playground at school. He yanks so hard that my tightly sealed lips jump right off his cock with a loud popping sound. My head is back again, I can feel a couple of promising drops land on my cheeks and my entire being is quivering with need and anticipation.

Also, I need to *know*. It's getting too much.

And he knows it too.

"You want to know who I am, Emma Carling, don't you?"

Is he bluffing? Do I want to come more than I want to see his face? Because if I see his face, that might very well kill the mood.

No! Grab the chance, you fool!

I'm breathing and thinking so hard that I forget to reply. He slaps me hard across the cheek. I reel from the shock more than the pain.

"Answer me," he says, barely whispering any more. His own power is running away with him. Just as it is with me.

And so I answer him, with words I didn't expect to escape my lips.

"Yes, Master. I want to see you, Master."

And I feel his fingers begin to tug at the knot of my blindfold.

End of Book 2

HER CALLING

THE EMMA SERIES, BOOK 3

In just a few short months the seductive, sexy and versatile Emma Carling has flourished into the undisputed champion of London high-class escorts. She's remained modest and generous despite her rise to wealth and fame. But it's not all plain sailing for the heroine of the *Emma* series in this concluding book.

In between threesome assignments, wicked scenes in nightclub bathrooms and a month in a tropical royal harem, she must also come to terms with betrayal, anxiety and even doubt. Can Emma conquer it all and take charge of her life? And can she use her incredible story to change other women's destinies for the better?

To buy this third paperback of the Emma series, head to jamesgreyauthor.com

CONNECTING WITH JAMES GREY

I suggest your first port of call be my official website at jamesgreyauthor.com. It's the best place to learn all about me and my work — and it's the *only* place to order those coveted signed paperbacks!

To connect with my community of fans and I, Facebook's ideal. So make a request to join the James Grey Fan Group. That's where I bounce cover ideas, run reader polls, take requests and announce my news first!

I love fan mail! Just like I love constructive criticism, meeting prospective beta readers or even hearing your fantasies. You can write to me via my website contact form.

Finally, I'd like to encourage you to join my mailing list. I'm planning some exclusive Emma-related content for my subscribers in the near future! Bear in mind too that I am at the mercy of the digital bookstores, and *they don't tell me who you are*. They could even decide to ban me overnight without warning (it happens!), destroying my livelihood and all the years of work to build up a fan base. If I have your email, at least I can find you again! For this scenario as much as anything else, won't you consider signing up via my website?

ALSO BY JAMES GREY

The Laura Series:

Out of Office (Book 1)

Playing Dirty (Book 2)

The Pleasure Studio (Book 3)

~

Novellas:

Hot Wet Touches

Hot Wet Touches Amsterdam

The Sex Club Diaries

Urge to Stray

~

Short Story Collections:

Breaking Free

Ravenous Desires

~

Choose Your Own Adventure Erotica:

Her Desire Awakened

~

This Series (Emma):

Escort in Training (Book 1)

Her Calling (Book 3)

Access all titles and formats via jamesgreyauthor.com.

ABOUT JAMES GREY

He may write his erotica under a nom-de-plume, but James Grey has been widely published by magazines and newspapers around the world. He still spends much of his working life writing about topics other than hardcore sex. This includes a series of travel books.

Grey began writing erotica in the run-up to Christmas 2013, inspired by a recent visit to a mixed, nude sauna in Germany and prompted by a subsequent period of ennui at his aunt's house in France. His self-published author ego was born a few days later, on a grim, hung-over New Year's Day in England, when he uploaded *Hot Wet Touches* to leading ebook platforms.

And since so many people ask: no, the author name he picked has nothing to do with *Fifty Shades*!

Grey has gone on to become a regular category best-seller in the biggest store of them all, and is one of only a handful of men writing erotica. Connect with him online, and you might even find a picture of the well-travelled Grey at a book signing event.

Grey lives in a European capital city. And sure, he's a little secretive when it comes to real-life identities and locations. Wouldn't you be too, if you'd written down your most sensual, intimate adventures for the world to read? But if you want to know something, why not simply ask him? ;)

www.jamesgreyauthor.com

ACKNOWLEDGMENTS

Oh my, where do I even begin?

I guess I'll start with you, dear reader. Thank you for buying this book – you've helped me to eat! And thanks for every like, share, review and wild raving about my signed copies. Remember, your seal of approval counts for everything in the book world.

Lori, thank you for your patience. And thanks too for all the stunning bookmarks, the grumpy 2am takeovers, those beautiful Excel spreadsheets (!) and the crisis management. I won't forget you being with me in the most troubled of times, and your sticking on my side. You too, Sharon…you deserve wonderful things, and thanks so much for inspiring me.

Debs, you have been a star for your teasers, your help with sexy cover pictures and your role as Senior Tax Affairs Officer. The IRS still makes me want to seek out a tall building every time I hear its name, but you've helped me handle it all a little better than I might have done.

Kelly, you've been a true friend and I can't thank you enough. Well done for nagging me to get to a signing – Dublin was surely the start of something! You are far too generous and kind to me, you've been an absolute blessing and you are…umm…usually right.

Thanks to all you bloggers who keep on letting the world know I exist. The online book world was a bewildering, bombarding, higgledy-piggledy place to me at first, and I've probably not communicated as I should have done. But now that I've finally started to put names to faces and figure out who *you* all are, I'm looking forward to truly knowing you.

Thanks to my parents for encouraging me to read when the other kids my age were content with chucking sand at each other. The same goes for everyone who has ever affirmed that I should write, from my first English teachers at school to my university lecturers. I have doubts about this business every single day, and you've all helped to silence them in your own way.

I must thank the dozens of magazine and newspaper editors who have published the writing I've done in other fields. You've paid me to write, and that's sent an important message about what I should be doing in life. I should also thank the editors (many of them the same people!) who couldn't answer a pitch email or take a phone call. Your silences are what led me to writing directly for my readers via self-publishing. I hope that it will prove to be the best move I have ever made.

Thanks to those who have beta-read my stories, and thanks also to Ida at Amygdala Design for some wonderful work on my covers. To my fellow authors who have shared your wisdom and experiences with me, thank you so much and let's keep doing it!

I should also thank the man upstairs for creating woman. Without the fairer sex, my life and my writing would be stricken. It seems I can never grow tired of womankind, and I cherish each encounter I have with you. You spellbind me, and I'm so glad I can put that feeling down in words for a living each day. Good job, Mr God!

More of you will come along and shower me with support, I'm sure. It just keeps on happening. And every time it does, it's a reminder that my writing makes a difference to people. Thanks in advance for those reminders. They make me carry on with this crazy, wonderful life.